Smoking Barrels

When Steve Hardie arrives in Cripple Creek, he finds himself involved in a scuffle with a bunch of drunken cowpokes. He bravely saves the life of the local sheriff but accidentally kills one of the cowboys. Because nobody kills one of Hyram Slade's men and lives, Hardie saddles up and leaves town.

However, the crazed Slade gathers up his hired henchmen and is in quick pursuit. Now only the death of the drifter will satisfy him.

In a face-to-face confrontation with Slade death beckons Steve. Can he live to see another day?

By the same author

Appaloosa King
The Forty Riders
Treacherous Trail

Smoking Barrels

John Ladd

A Black Horse Western

ROBERT HALE · LONDON

© John Ladd 2011
First published in Great Britain 2011

ISBN 978-0-7090-9177-6

Robert Hale Limited
Clerkenwell House
Clerkenwell Green
London EC1R 0HT

www.halebooks.com

Typeset by
Derek Doyle & Associates, Shaw Heath
Printed and bound in Great Britain by
CPI Antony Rowe, Chippenham and Eastbourne

Dedicated to Carol Bowen.
Still blonde and still beautiful.

PROLOGUE

There was a certain breed of men in what was eventually to be called the Wild West. A breed that lived by an unwritten code which was branded into their very souls. A code of honour. Perhaps it was something they had always had or something they had learned for themselves as they grew up in the untamed stretches of land beyond the Pecos. These men never did to others what they would not wish done to them. As long as you left them alone and did neither them or their kin any harm, they would remain passive. Yet just one inch over that invisible line drawn in the sand and you could provoke them into becoming the most fearsome of foes.

Mostly this special breed of men looked no different from any other two-legged creature. Some did draw attention to themselves like flies to an outhouse by their very nature, but they were cut from the same cloth as their quieter brothers.

They would never hurt anyone unless provoked. Never start a fight either with fist or with gun but were always willing to finish one. Some said that Steve Hardie was such a man. He was never a soul to seek out attention and he remained quiet for most of the time he lived and breathed.

Few ever saw him lose his temper but those who did never forgot what they witnessed.

Still a long way short of his thirtieth birthday, Hardie had no ties to hold him to any one place. There had not been any sweethearts to rope him since the end of the war. No kinfolk were left to keep him in any one place long enough for roots to set down.

Hardie had become a drifter. A cowpuncher when he needed to chow down and earn a little trail money. A deputy when he was even more in need of money. Anything you wanted doing, Steve Hardie was always willing to do unless it broke that unwritten code he lived by.

It was a lonely existence. One which allowed for few possessions apart from a twin-rigged pair of .45s and a black gelding. Yet the tall drifter had never coveted things the way most men do. As long as he had enough food for himself and his loyal horse he was a happy man, content to camp out under the stars as he vainly searched for that place few of us ever find. A place where we might be persuaded to permanently hang up our spurs and finally settle down.

Steve Hardie did not harm others unless they were foolish enough to try and harm him.

Men who live by that unwritten code are a dangerous breed to get riled up. Steve Hardie was no exception.

The sun was beginning to set as church bells began to toll through Cripple Creek. It was as though they were ringing out an ominous warning of what was about to happen. The drifter glanced from his high perch atop the black gelding at men and women in their Sunday best as they headed churchward in answer to the bells' summons. He reined in and brushed the dust from his clothes as other men and women aimed their boots toward the main street's array of saloons and gambling halls. Two very different types of people greeting the coming of nightfall in two very different ways. The drifter wanted no part of either group.

Steve Hardie was tired. Dog tired. It had been a long ride from Yuma to this fleabitten settlement set in the lowest part of a valley between two mountain peaks. The grass had been sweet and nourishing for the last quarter of his long trek and that had satisfied Hardie's trusty mount.

The drifter turned the horse towards the nearest hitching rail and tapped his spurs. The obedient animal walked to the twisted pole, then waited as its master looped a leg over its head and slid silently to the ground. Hardie was a man of few words and actions. He just travelled where the trail led him looking for just enough work to fill his belly for a few weeks. He had never wanted to make his fortune as so many others did. Hardie was satisfied if he just managed to have enough money to buy an inch-thick steak whenever the urge came to him.

The drifter looked around the street. It was wide and straight, as though the folks who had planned this town had actually given it more than just a passing thought. He led the horse close to a trough and secured his reins to the hitching pole. The horse dropped its head and started to drink as its master looked all around him. Everything seemed quiet and few even noticed the stranger within the boundaries of their town.

That suited Hardie. He never wanted trouble and would go a long way to avoid it. He patted the horse's neck.

The sky was going red as the sun set over the nearest of the mountain peaks. There were enough clouds up there to make a strange pattern across the big stretch of the heavens as he gazed up. He did not like the look of it. Since the end of the war Hardie had been consumed by superstitions. Once he had believed in something else, just like those who were making their way to the church, but that had been before he had seen what war could do to men, women and innocent children. Faith had been replaced by a simpler consideration. Like the Indians who had once filled this vast land he believed in signs. Omens. Whatever handle you liked to hang on them, Steve Hardie gave them all due thought.

The drifter had eaten little since he had set out for Cripple Creek apart from hard tack and the occasional cooked meal whenever he got lucky and managed to catch a jack rabbit for the skillet that he carried in his saddle-bag.

Hardie inhaled deeply.

Fried chicken sure smelled good after a diet of badly burned vittles and jaw-breaking biscuits. He stepped up on to the boardwalk and again tried to dust himself down as he looked in through the window of the small café.

Removing his Stetson the drifter turned the door-knob and entered the café. It was no more than twelve feet square but somehow had six round tables within its walls. At the far wall there was a gap, from where the aroma of cooking came. He hung his hat on the tall stand, made his way to a table and pulled out one of its chairs. Hardie sat down.

A rotund man with a white apron wrapped around his girth appeared and closed the distance between them.

'What'll it be, stranger?'

'Do I smell chicken frying, pard?' Hardie asked.

'Yep.' The man smiled.

'I'll have me a whole one with a side order of potatoes.'

'Coffee?'

Hardie smiled wide. 'Thank ya kindly.'

That had been less than an hour ago, but every scrap of food had been consumed by the weary drifter. Only well-sucked chicken bones remained. Hardie poured the last of the coffee from the pot into his cup and swallowed the black beverage. Then he heard something which drew his attention to the door. It was the sound of men laughing loudly out on the boardwalk. Hardie narrowed his eyes and focused out beyond the café's glass panes. Street lanterns had already been lit; they cast an eerie amber glow over the entire street. At first the drifter paid no attention until he heard the familiar sound of his horse.

Something was wrong.

Hardie swiftly rose and tossed a silver dollar on to the chequered tablecloth. He turned and adjusted his twin-holstered shooting-rig, then strode towards the door. He plucked his Stetson from the stand, placed it on his head, then snatched the doorknob and opened the door.

The drifter stared towards his horse and the four cowboys who were gathered around it. The horse was vainly pulling at its tethers as the cowboys roared with drunken laughter.

For a moment Hardie did not say a word. He just

stood silently in the light that spilled from the café and watched them. A fiery fury was erupting inside him, though.

Oblivious to their onlooker, two of the cowboys were taking great pleasure in using their knives to cut into the tethered horse's flanks. Hardie saw the blood and acted.

He strode to the edge of the boardwalk.

'What the hell are ya doing?' he snarled.

The drunken cowpunchers turned their attention to the tall man, who appeared even taller as he stood on the boardwalk above them.

One of their number was sober enough to turn on his heels and run off back to the nearest saloon. The other three glared up at Hardie. The pair with the bloody knives in their hands waved their blades at him.

'Lookee there,' one of them mocked. 'Better go run away, sonny, before we cuts ya gizzard out.'

One of the cowboys spat at the drifter. Spittle covered Hardie's pants legs. 'I reckon we oughta slice 'em both up, boys.'

'Big talk for a dwarf,' Hardie said with a snarl.

'What ya call me?' The cowpoke rushed forward.

Mustering every scrap of his energy, Hardie kicked out and caught the man's chin with the tip of his left boot. Teeth flew in all directions before the cowboy fell like a sack of lead into the sand.

'Let's get him.'

'Damn right.'

The two cowboys with the knives in their hands started to slash at the air between them and the drifter. Hardie felt the honed blade of one of their weapons catch his pants leg. Blood ran down from the gash into his boot.

Without thinking of his own safety the drifter threw himself off the boardwalk and at the men. With his arms outstretched Hardie caught both of his targets around their necks. All three crashed into the shadows at the hoofs of the distressed gelded black. The terrified horse tried to rear up but his reins kept him firmly secured to the hitching pole. The crazed animal leapt around as the drifter wrestled with the pair of cowboys. The hoofs came down, barely missing the three fighting men.

Hardie saw the blood-soaked blades flash in the amber light as both came seeking out his guts. He rolled over, then grabbed at the hands of both his adversaries. He grappled on the sand until he managed to force himself on to his knees. One of the men tore his hand free. Hardie smashed his free fist into the cowboy's jaw.

The cowboy slumped into the ground head first. Still holding the other man's knife hand firmly, the drifter swung around as the cowboy's fist crashed into his chin. His head rolled back. Hardie was stunned for a moment but managed to avoid the following punches of his attacker. Both men scrambled back to their feet as they continued to exchange blows. The cowboy head-butted Hardie with all his might. The drifter released his grip and staggered back a few steps. Then, as he saw the knife charging towards him in the cowboy's clenched hand, Hardie sidestepped and threw a powerful punch into the cowboy's guts. The knife fell to the sand as the cowboy buckled. Hardie clenched both hands together and brought his full strength down on the man's neck. The sound of the cowboys head hitting the side of the boardwalk echoed in Hardie's ears.

The drifter glanced at the three unconscious men scattered around him and was staggering back to his horse when his eyes espied a burly man wearing a tin star approaching him.

The sheriff rested knuckles on hips and tutted at the sight of the trio of unconscious cowpunchers. He then looked at Hardie long and hard.

'Ya lucky I seen it all, stranger,' Joe Daley said. He stepped down to the dusty street and kicked each of the cowboys in turn to satisfy himself that they were all out for the count. Then he looked at the bleeding horse. 'They do this to ya horse, boy?'

'Yep.' Hardie nodded.

'I'd have shot the varmints,' Daley admitted. 'Horseflesh is valuable in these parts.'

Suddenly, as if in response to the words which had just left the lawman's lips, a shot blasted out from the saloon just behind both men. It was the saloon in which the fourth of the cowboys had taken refuge.

A line of deafening white lightning cut through the air. Its heat was felt by both the sheriff and the drifter.

'What the hell?' Daley snarled.

Steve Hardie swung around and saw the cowboy cock and fire his gun again. Blood splattered over the drifter as the sheriff was hit. Faster than the wounded lawman had ever seen anyone move before, Hardie drew his guns and fired them both in unison. The cowboy was lifted off his feet and fell backwards. Dust rose from the boardwalk as the body landed limply upon its weathered surface.

Hardie holstered his guns and wrapped an arm around the bleeding sheriff. In seconds the street became filled with curious onlookers.

'I never seen anyone draw that fast before, boy,' Daley gasped. 'Thank ya.'

'Are ya hurt bad, Sheriff?' Hardie asked anxiously.

Daley straightened up. He was holding his shoulder, from where blood was coming between his fingers. He cleared his throat, then looked at the drifter.

'I bin hurt worse,' the sheriff said.

'I'll take ya to the doc if ya tell me where he is.'

'Forget that. I'd ride out of here if'n I was you, boy,' the sheriff advised. 'Ride out fast.'

Hardie was confused. 'Why?'

'Ya can't go killing no cowpokes around here.' Daley spoke with urgency. 'Listen up. Get going.'

'I don't cotton to this. He tried to kill you, Sheriff,' Hardie said. Bewilderment etched his features. 'I had to kill him or he'd have killed the both of us. Ya know that so why should I light out like a yella belly?'

Daley pushed himself away from his saviour and pulled the reins of the black gelding free of the hitching rail. The sheriff rammed the reins into Hardie's hands.

'Don't try to figure it. Ride, boy. Ride while ya still can,' the lawman insisted. 'Savvy?'

Steve Hardie gave a nod and threw himself up on to the back of the nervous horse. He did not understand why, but he spurred and thundered away into the darkness which surrounded the town known as Cripple Creek.

Still watching the dust kicked up from the hoofs of the galloping black mount as it hung in the dry air, Daley leaned against the hitching pole with blood pouring from between the fingers which were pressed into his shoulder wound.

The sheriff knew the curious crowd were closing in on him, and with them the reason for his fears.

'That poor critter's a dead man,' he muttered to himself. 'He just don't know it yet.'

ONE

It was hot and getting hotter with every passing beat of the drifter's pounding heart. There seemed to be no escape. Who were they? Why wouldn't they quit? Blistering rays of merciless sun cascaded down from the heavens above the horseman as he spurred and whipped his mount on and on into the sickening heat haze. The horse was spent but kept obeying its master's commands. The words of warning from Sheriff Joe Daley kept on returning to the fevered mind of the terrified horseman. The lawman seemed to be trying to tell him, for some reason that Hardie was unable to understand, that it was not smart to kill cowpokes in or around Cripple Creek.

The horse staggered and nearly fell but the man upon its saddle used all his power to drag rein and keep the animal on its feet. Hardie swung the tails of his long reins and cracked them across the horse's tail. Somehow the lathered-up black gelding responded again and started to cover the dry ground at pace once more. Hardie turned and looked back into the swirling dust. The fertile valley where he had camped the previous night was now little more than a memory. Now the ground was arid and stony and yet the faithful horse still obeyed its master. Still Hardie tried to find a speed that might allow them to lose the riflemen who kept on coming after them.

The dust kicked up from the hoofs of the black gelding hung in the dry air behind the fleeing rider. Even though the ground was too hard to leave tracks, the dust would give them away, Hardie feared.

Then, ahead, Hardie saw something. At first it seemed to be a field of precious jewels sparkling across the ground beyond the sagebrush and sun-bleached trees. As the gelded black got to it the reality of what Hardie's dust-filled eyes were straining at became obvious. It was a river. Shallow and wide. The drifter stood in his stirrups and studied what lay beyond the fast-flowing water.

Massive boulders stood along the riverbank for as far as he could see in either direction. They were smooth and looked as though some unseen giant's hands must have placed them there because there was no other explanation Hardie's weary mind could think of. They rose higher than the drifter could have imagined possible.

Beyond them he could see one of the mountain peaks, rising jagged and defiant against time. Hardie again leaned to his side and looked back. Through a gap in the dust which still lingered above the arid terrain he saw them again. They were still coming, he thought fearfully. Still hell-bent on killing him. Hardie swung back to face what lay ahead of him.

The shallow river spanned more than 200 yards from the brushland to the rocky outcrop. Most times finding a river of crystal-clear water was something a drifter could only hope for. It would be regarded as a gift from whatever gods you rode with. Now it seemed to be nothing more than another obstacle to try and overcome.

The rider forced himself back up until he was balanced like a tightrope walker in his stirrups. The unyielding sun, now directly overhead, seemed to blind both horse and rider as they reached the lapping edge of the embankment.

Hardie hauled rein and the mount stopped. The drifter twisted again on his saddle and looked back into the clouds of dust he had created. As his gelding lowered its head and started to drink, Hardie listened.

Even the dust could not shield the drifter from the fear which refused to leave him. The sound of the pounding hoofs of his pursuers was echoing all around him.

They were still coming.

They sounded to the drifter like messengers from Hell. He turned back to gaze across the wide stretch of water before him. Hardie hauled on the reins of his drinking mount and shook his head. He knew that the faithful horse was finished and yet they had no time to rest. No time to waste. They had to keep going. Keep trying to find a place which would protect them from the bullets of the rifle-toting riders.

He yelled out and rammed his spurs back. The black horse responded by jumping into the river. It started to negotiate its fast-flowing waters. Spray rose over both rider and horse. It was icy cold. Hardie knew that the river must be flowing from that distant mountain. He kept spurring and continuing to thrash the shoulders of the exhausted horse with the tails of his reins. For more than two hours he had been trying to outrun the men who were after him. Now, heading towards what he hoped might be a sanctuary, he wondered whether his worn-out horse could reach the opposite bank before the riflemen got to the water's edge. The range of their Winchesters was far greater than the width of the river. If his pursuers got to the river before he reached the other bank, they would easily pluck him from his saddle with their deadly lead.

Hardie kept urging the flagging creature beneath his saddle onwards as his eyes narrowed and focused on the wall of boulders. Again the drifter's wearied mind thought about giants having created the awe-inspiring scenery. How else could so many massive stones have become balanced upon one another if not placed there by some unseen giant hand?

Suddenly the horse slowed and then stopped. It was at last out of the strength which had carried them to this point. Hardie tried to encourage it on with spurs and reins but the gelding had nothing left.

The drifter looped his leg over its head and slid down into the rushing water. It came up to Hardie's knees as he moved to the wide-eyed horse's head.

He grabbed the bridle and tugged hard. For a moment the creature simply did not move. Hardie leaned back until the water was soaking the back of his shirt.

'C'mon!' The drifter's voice was strained.

Like the horse, Hardie also wanted to stop and rest. Yet he knew that to stop would be to allow the long rifles of those who chased him to find their range. So far he had been lucky. Damn lucky. None of their bullets had come close either to him or to his exhausted horse. But luck has always been a two-sided coin. It has bad as well as good sides and to stop now in midstream meant almost certain death.

'C'mon!' Hardie screamed out again as he desperately pulled at the bridle of the sorrowful-looking horse in a vain attempt to get the animal moving. The drifter stood back up to his full height and sucked in a lungful of air as his squinting eyes sought out the riflemen who, he knew, were now closer than they had ever been. 'Ya gonna get us both killed if'n ya don't start walking, boy.'

Then the menacing sound rang out again. The sound of rifles unleashing their lethal fury.

Three or four Winchester bullets kicked up the water twenty feet behind the man and his horse. Hardie gritted his teeth and glared back into the swirling clouds of dust that his horse had left in its wake before reaching the river.

Then he saw them. It felt as though his heart had suddenly stopped pounding inside his chest. The only good thing in his favour was that they were still at least a quarter of a mile behind him.

But they were getting closer with every stride of their horses' powerful legs. For hours Hardie had wondered how they could have kept up their relentless pace whilst his own mount had become drained of almost every last scrap of its strength. Then he saw the answer.

Each of the riders was leading a spare saddle horse. Hardie swallowed hard in disbelief. How could they be so well prepared, he thought? How?

What did it matter? They were. That was all that counted. They were. A panic washed over him as chilling as the icy waters in which he stood. He wanted to fire back and stop them, but knew that if their Winchesters did not have the range to reach him, then his .45s would fall well short of their targets.

The gelding suddenly gave out a pitiful whinny and took a few faltering steps. Had the few moments' rest helped the black horse get its second breath? There was only one way the drifter was going to find out.

Hardie grabbed his saddle horn and thrust his boot into the nearer stirrup. He pulled himself out of the water and dropped on to his saddle. His right boot soon found the other stirrup as another crescendo of bullets rocked the air around him. The water kicked up as lead balls smashed into it on both sides.

'Damn it all. Now they got our range,' Hardie cursed.

Their shots rattled out again.

This time they sounded louder. This time he saw the water ahead of them cut up as the bullets came down. Plumes of water rose into the air.

He tried to stand in his stirrups but his legs were as tired as his horse's. There was only one thing to do. Duck and get the hell out of the river before the next volley tore him to shreds.

Hardie screamed out, he swirled his reins over his horse's head and rammed both his spurs into the animal's flanks. There was no mercy in the drifter now. Now he had to be brutal if he were to steer both of them out of reach of the men who were dedicated to killing them.

The bedraggled animal managed to labour on through the water's strong current. Each step of the spent creature brought them closer and closer to their goal: dry land. That was all the drifter could think of. Getting his horse back on to dry ground before a rifle shell found its target.

It felt like an eternity but in truth was only a matter of seconds before Hardie managed to achieve his goal. The gelding staggered out on to dry ground and swayed like a drunkard as it tried to maintain its balance.

The wall of smooth, rounded rocks before them looked far bigger than Hardie had imagined them to be but he was grateful for that small mercy. There were a score of trails leading in between the rocks. The horseman dragged back on his reins and swiftly dropped to the ground.

His legs buckled beneath him, yet he managed to remain upright. He grabbed the reins even more tightly and held the sorrowful-looking creature in check.

Hardie narrowed his eyes and gritted his teeth as he looked back at the pursuers. They had almost reached the river. Hardie knew that he could lie on his belly and pick them off one by one when they started to cross the river, but that was not his way. So far neither side had spilled any blood.

Who were they?

The question had dogged him since sunup.

Why were they after him?

He thought about the events back at Cripple Creek, and the strange warning by the sheriff. A chill traced his spine. Were they out to make him pay for killing that cowpoke?

His narrowed eyes spotted the white foaming water rise at the opposite bank as some of the horsemen guided their mounts into the river. He drew one of his guns and pulled back its hammer until it fully locked in position. He squeezed the trigger. The deafening shot was followed by four more.

The drifter felt a wry smile etch his features when he saw the riders retreat to dry land.

'Good,' Hardie drawled. 'Stay there awhile.'

He needed to buy time to figure out what to do next.

Hardie grabbed his empty canteen, unscrewed its stopper and lowered it into the river's cold water. When he judged it to be full he pulled it up and secured its stopper again.

Then a volley of bullets filled the dry air. Suddenly chunks of rock were being chipped off the boulders behind him. He was showered in dust. The pursuers still had the advantage of range with their long repeating trifles, he thought.

'Better get going, boy,' Hardie said to the dripping horse beside him. 'It ain't healthy around here.'

The lone horseman hung the canteen back on the horn of his saddle and tightened his grip on the reins. The gelded black wanted no part of continuing but Hardie forced the tired animal on. He led his mount into the nearest of the gaps between the gigantic rocks and kept going.

Somehow he had to get the pair of them to the top of the rocks and see if there was a chance of finding a place where they might either hide or at least use to their advantage.

The horse was in a bad way. Hardie knew that he should never have ridden it the way he had, and normally he would not have done so, but then folks did not normally chase and try to kill them with repeating rifles.

Each step was agony to the weary horseman as he led the horse higher and higher up into the maze of small trails between the huge rocks. High-heeled boots were fine to keep a man's feet firmly in his stirrups but they were not designed for walking any distance.

He could no longer see his followers as he laboured on up into the shadows of the winding trails but he could sure hear their weaponry. The sound of their shots echoed all around Hardie. He staggered onwards and upwards, leading the pitifully weak horse which, he knew, might have burst its heart if he had not dismounted when he had.

Hardie kept looking back but now all there was to

see were the rounded sides of rocks so big they defied imagination. He felt like an insect compared to their magnitude. Some were balanced from one side of the narrow trail to the other. He knew that if one of them fell it would crush everything beneath it.

The shots rang out again.

Yet now he no longer shook whenever he heard the venomous volley of the Winchesters. At least now he was safe until they caught up with him, he thought.

How long would it be before they mustered their courage and risked crossing the river? He hoped it would be well after sundown. Steve Hardie knew he could cover a lot of ground in the five or six hours left between now and the coming of nightfall.

He was panting long and hard.

Air was almost non-existent within the confines of the maze of granite. After what felt like the longest ten minutes of his entire life, Hardie stopped and dragged his Stetson from his head. Sweat flowed over his face, burning his eyes with salt.

'Thirsty?' he asked the horse, dropping the hat down before the sad-looking creature he knew he had almost killed. He filled the bowl of the hat with water, then took a quick swig before returning the canteen back to the saddle horn. The animal drank slowly as if it were too tired to even swallow.

Hardie used the time to reload his guns. He only

used them once in the previous six months. Both weapons needed greasing but there was no time for that. No time to do anything but ensure that all their cylinders were loaded with fresh bullets.

The drifter tried to work out what had happened to him a short while after sunrise. It was all so unbelievable that it seemed like a nightmare. Yet Hardie knew that this was no nightmare. He would not awaken from this to find nothing more than a sweat-soaked trail blanket to trouble him.

Why had the riders chosen him to vent their fury upon?

The question had come repeatedly to his mind but he had found no answer. He had just been trying to stay alive until this moment. He ran his fingers through his wet sandy-coloured hair and felt a chill trace his spine under his soaked shirt.

'Who are they?' Hardie asked the horse as it finished drinking and he was able to pluck his hat up off the ground and put it back on his head. 'What they want with me? It has gotta be something to do with that cowpuncher I killed. Gotta be.'

The horse snorted as though answering its master.

'C'mon, boy.' Hardie grabbed the bridle and began to lead the horse on up into what looked the way to the highest point of the rocks.

Both horse and master kept on up their slow climb. The further they went the higher the boulders to each side seemed to be stacked. There was a cold chill here where the sun was unable to reach. The sides of the smooth boulders gleamed with green lichen.

The drifter and his joyless mount ignored their pain and kept on ascending the trail.

There was nothing else they could do.

TWO

Cattle rancher Hyram Slade was a man who had more than his fair share of secrets hidden in the depths of his dark soul. He had never seemed to be short either of cash or of anything else he desired. His herd of longhorn steers stretched across every inch of the fertile land which surrounded Cripple Creek. There had been many rumours about the muscular Slade since he had first arrived with guns blazing a decade earlier in the once peaceful area. None was ever spoken aloud.

Where once there had been a dozen or more smaller ranches dotted around the rich, sweet-grassed range, now there was only one. And it was called the Lazy S. The Lazy S belonged to the brutal Slade. Ten years earlier the man, who claimed to be a Virginian, had arrived with a half-dozen gunhands in tow and fifty steers of various brands. It had not taken long for the rugged Slade to see off all his rivals, until he ruled not only the range but everything else within its unmarked boundaries. Some said he owned the entire county and there were few who dared argue the point within earshot of Slade or any of his so-called cowboys.

To rule with an iron fist was a saying brought to the West from lands far away but it fitted the rancher like a well-tailored suit. Slade ruled like an ancient monarch from the Dark Ages of Europe. He had not one merciful bone in his entire being and he liked it that way. His herd was now numbered in their thousands and the people of Cripple Creek knew how Slade had managed to create his prosperous empire. Nearly every steer that graced the range had been rustled from legitimate ranchers' stock and driven here from all directions.

Each of their hides had been subjected to the expertise of hot irons in the hands of Slade's brand-burners. There was not a single brand which the rancher's brand-burners could not alter to become identical to the Lazy S mark.

With cattle fetching record prices in Dodge and all the other railhead towns, Hyram Slade had seen his fortune grow at such a rate that he could no longer calculate his own wealth.

Most men who had managed to achieve so much in such a short period of time might have been satisfied to sit back and just wallow in their own fortune, but not Slade. The ruthless rancher had never been able to rid himself of the black demonic nature which had festered inside him since he had killed his first man.

Slade had become so intoxicated by his own grip on power that he refused to allow anyone to question him or his motives for anything. The gunslinger remained within his craw, gnawing at his innards like cheap liquor and never satisfied.

Power corrupts. That was true of Hyram Slade. The old saying might as well have been carved into his flesh. He would not allow anyone to show any backbone. If they did he would happily cut it out and chew on its bloody length.

He ruled for as far as he could see. The citizens of Cripple Creek knew that all too well. He owned them just as he owned everything else. There was no real law in the land he dominated, apart from that which he had created himself.

So it had been on the previous night when the rancher, flanked by a dozen of his top hired guns, had ridden into Cripple Creek's main thoroughfare from his ranch beyond the lush swaying grass to the town's eastern border. News of the drifter having killed one of Slade's men had reached the rancher's ears within an hour of the event.

Roaring like a raging bull, Slade had saddled up and brought part of his small army with him to administer his own brand of justice.

Even though the rancher always referred to his

men as cowboys every eye that watched them as they trooped into the town knew what they really were.

Each and every one of them was nothing more than a heartless killer, exactly like their leader.

The rancher and his followers had drawn rein outside the offices of Doc Carter, having been informed that the wounded Sheriff Daley had been taken there to have the bullet cut out of his shoulder.

Slade dismounted and tossed his reins to the only man he knew to be as ruthless as he was himself. Flint Colby accepted the leathers and watched his boss kick his way into the lantern-lit office like a rabid animal.

'Daley!' the rancher yelled out loudly.

Doc Carter came from the rear room. Blood still covered the doctor's hands as evidence of what he had been doing only moments before.

'Mr Slade,' Carter said in greeting. He seated himself down at his desk, pulled a cork from his half-consumed whiskey bottle and took two long swallows from its neck. 'What can I do for ya?'

Slade pointed at the door to the back room. 'Daley in there, Doc?'

Carter gave a slow nod and returned the bottle neck to his lips. He watched as the rancher forged powerfully into the rear of the small building.

Slade stood over the table where Daley lay on his shirtless back. The stitching on the sheriff's fleshy

shoulder was crude but effective. The rancher's eyes
darted about until they kit upon the small enamel
kidney bowl. Its white was stained with red and a
lump of lead lay beside forceps.

The sheriff tilted his head sideways and looked up
at the fearsome sight loomed over him.

'I'm sorry, Mr Slade,' Daley croaked weakly.

'Ya sorry?' Slade showed no mercy and grabbed
the hair of the injured lawman. He lifted Daley's
head off the table and shook it with a fevered frenzy.
'Ya let one of my cowboys get killed, Joe. Sorry ain't
fitting. Sorry don't cut the mustard this time. Brady
got killed and ya let it happen.'

Daley was terrified. His eyes watered as the
rancher shook his head by the hair before dropping
it once again. The hard surface of the table did not
give as the sheriff's head bumped upon it.

'It was a drifter that done it,' Daley managed to
say.

Slade leaned over until his eyes were so close to
the terrified sheriff's that neither man could focus.
'A drifter? Ya let a stinking drifter gun down my
man? Ya should have killed that drifter, Joe. Killed
him dead.'

'It weren't like that, Mr Slade.' There was desperation in the sheriff's voice. 'Ya boy Brady and some
of his pals had started to cut up the drifter's horse
outside the café. The drifter had a fight with three
of 'em. Brady had run off into the Horseshoe saloon

when the punches started to fly and when the fight stopped he opened up on me and the drifter with his hogleg.'

'Brady shot ya?' Slade growled in disbelief.

'Honest Injun,' Daley said. 'That's what happened. Brady plugged me and the drifter just acted in self-defence. Ya boy would have done for the both of us if that young stranger hadn't have gotten the better of him.'

'What was his name, this drifter who saved ya worthless bacon, Joe?' Slade boomed.

Daley's head shook. 'I dunno.'

'Ya let him kill Brady and ya didn't ask him his name?'

'I was hurting real bad.'

'OK. Then where'd he go?'

'He headed west out of town. Towards the range and the prairie, I reckon.' The sheriff watched as the glowering Slade straightened up.

'Why'd ya let him go for, Joe?' Slade asked.

'It was self-defence, Mr Slade,' Daley stammered. 'I had nothing to hold him for.'

'Ya shouldn't have let him go, Joe.' The rancher looked at the tray filled with surgical instruments. All of them were covered in the sheriff's gore. Slade ran a gloved finger across them until he found a scalpel. 'Ya really shouldn't have let that varmint go. Ya knows that. That drifter gotta be punished. Gotta have his neck stretched.'

'I . . . I was shot, Mr Slade. I couldn't have stopped him from leaving town.' Daley heard the sound of the scalpel being lifted from the tray. Fear swept over the sheriff. He had seen what the rancher could and would do many times in the past. Daley tried to move but then felt the hand on his bloodstained chest holding him down. 'What ya doing, Mr Slade?'

Slade raised the scalpel and looked at its sharp blade glinting in the lamplight. A strange smile crossed the rancher's face as he turned the honed instrument round until its blade was aimed downwards.

'Learning ya a lesson, Joe,' the cold voice replied. 'Ya gotta be punished just like I'm gonna have to punish that drifter who done for Brady. Folks don't respect a man like me if'n they ain't feared. Savvy?'

There was no time for the lawman to utter even the shortest of replies.

Daley felt the scalpel being driven into his chest the first time the gloved hand pounded down. But as the blade punctured the sheriff's heart, Daley felt nothing more. Not one of the following dozen or more equally accurate and frenzied blows delivered by the snarling Slade.

Doc Carter looked up at the rancher as the big man came out of the back room. He said nothing as he saw the bloody scalpel being discarded. He simply nodded when Slade had instructed him to bury his patient.

That had been a whole lifetime ago to Hyram Slade as he sat astride his horse amid his army of gunfighters on the banks of the wide river staring out at the wall of boulders and the mountain range beyond. Now all he could think about was catching the man who had got the better of one of his highly paid henchmen. The sun was high and hot now.

The rancher sat atop his lathered-up horse as Colby eased his own mount close to his paymaster. 'We gonna wait here until sundown before we head on across, boss?'

Slade did not answer the question. His burning red eyes just kept staring out across the fast-flowing river. There was vengeance fermenting inside his guts and he knew that there was only one way it could be satisfied.

'Boss?' Colby ventured.

'I ain't feared. I ain't waiting for stinking nightfall like some yella bastard.' Slade spurred his horse and drove it into the river. 'C'mon. We got us a varmint to skin and kill.'

The dozen riders followed.

THREE

Plumes of water rose and hung defiantly in the air above the charging line of riders as they ploughed through the river. The cowpunchers had crossed its wide expanse in a flurry of excitement and ruthless determination. These were men who no longer just wished to catch the elusive Steve Hardie. Now they wanted to kill him, to earn the bonus Hyram Slade had promised his henchmen. His madness had somehow infected all of their minds like a wildfire. Perhaps it was because they wanted to put an end to this long chase and head on back home.

Killing the fleeing Hardie would achieve that goal. It would satisfy Slade and the bloodlust with which he had managed to inject their heartless souls. It had to end soon. It would end with gun-smoke and retribution.

Each rider led his spare mount through the ice-cold water and did not quit spurring until he had reached the opposite bank. Only then did the men draw rein and allow their horses to catch their wind.

Colby considered the gigantic rounded rocks before them with eyes which never fully opened, as though he were always squinting at his next chosen target. This time he was studying the unusual terrain with innocent eyes. He, like nearly all of the men who had ridden with Slade to this point, had never been to this strange place previously. Never encountered the monolith which now faced them.

The sun was high and getting hotter with every passing moment. Steam rose all around the horses as its rays of blistering heat dried water from their flanks. Shimmering haze swirled all around them. The trails between the boulders were in dark shadow and uninviting. Few sane men would ever have willingly chosen to ride up into the unknown from where the steaming horses stood.

Flint Colby looked along the length of the impressive wall of boulders and at the many gaps set between them. To his surprise some of the trails up into the rocks were big enough to drive wagons through. Others were narrow and daunting. But which one of the countless trails had their quarry taken? The damp reddish ground was cut up by the incessant lapping of the river as it sped along its ancient course. Hardly an inch of the soil had not been lashed and that which had escaped the river's rage was being cut up by Slade's horsemen.

'Anything, Flint? Ya see anything?' Slade asked his top gun frantically as he loaded his Winchester for the umpteenth time.

Colby swung his mount round and shook his head in answer. 'He could have taken any one of them trails up into the high country, Slade. He could be up there waiting to pick us off one by one for all I knows.'

The rancher gritted his teeth and took a deep, noisy breath. It was like the roar of a caged lion. He was furious with everything and everyone.

'Damn it all,' Slade cursed. He glared hard at the gunfighter. 'Which 'un do ya think he took, Flint?'

Flint Colby had never been frightened of any man he had ever encountered but Slade was a different kettle of fish. Slade had an insanity about him which even fast-drawing shootists were wary of. Men like Slade could go from quiet and calm to totally loco in a matter of seconds and Colby had witnessed that very change. The slightest seemingly unimportant thing could send the rancher into blind rages which made the man kill. Colby knew that the hapless Sheriff Daley had paid the ultimate price back at Cripple Creek for simply not being good enough to prevent the shoot-out which had claimed the cowpuncher's life. Colby had worked for Slade for more years than he cared to recall but even that meant nothing to the rancher. He would vent his anger on anyone, even kin, when his dander was up.

'I figure he must have reached this point.' Colby pointed a finger at the ground. It was a guess but one he knew would satisfy his paymaster. The gunfighter pointed at the nearest gap in the wall of rocks knowingly. 'By my figuring that means he must have cut up into this trail here.'

Hyram Slade looked at where Colby's finger was aimed. He thought about it for a while, then gave a quick nod of his head. 'Yeah. Ya right. He must have lit up through there. The stinking yella dog must be trying to put distance between himself and us. Ain't gonna work, though. Ya hear me? It ain't gonna work.'

Colby swung the head of his tired horse away from Slade and gave a silent sigh. He had managed to convince the man of something which he did not actually believe himself. 'Yep. We hear ya, boss.'

Slade leaned back and looked up. It was impossible to see anything except the boulders which were balanced upon one another in a seemingly gravity-defying manner. The reflection of the bright sun blinded all eyes from further investigation. The rancher looked at his men in turn. Each felt the cold chill of doubt trace their spines beneath their sodden shirts.

'Where do these trails lead, Flint?' asked Dan Foster. He was a relatively new member of Slade's army of cowpunchers.

Colby shrugged.

'To Cooper's Falls,' Slade told him waving his rifle.

'What's that?' another of the cowboys, called Slim Peters, wondered aloud.

'A waterfall,' Slade replied. 'The biggest damn waterfall ya ever done seen. Comes right off the top of the mountain over yonder. Fed by solid ice from its peak. Leastways, that's what folks reckon. I only bin up there once when I first come to this country. Mighty high waterfall that feeds this and a dozen other rivers hereabouts.'

Colby noticed a smile on Slade's hardened features. He had seen that sickening hyena-like expression before. Slade did not have a sense of humour. When he smiled it intimated a darker, more menacing mood. 'What ya thinking about, boss? Ya looks plumb amused by something.'

'I do?' Slade eased himself off his horse and looped his leathers around the saddle horn of his second-string mount. He slid the loaded Winchester into its scabbard, grabbed hold of the horse's mane and stepped into the stirrup. He hauled himself up on to his relatively fresh mount and gathered up its reins.

'Yep. Ya do.' Colby pushed the brim of his Stetson off his temple. A red line remained on his tanned brow. 'What ya got brewing inside ya head?'

'Well, let me inform ya as to the facts of Cooper's Falls, Flint.' Slade leaned back against his saddle cantle.

The other cowboys followed Slade's lead and changed mounts as their boss imparted his knowledgeable information to them in a dry low drawl.

'These trails all lead up to one place. A flat ridge up on the top of these boulders. Ain't nothing up there but wild critters.'

'And?' Colby pressed.

'And nothing.' Slade nodded firmly. 'Fifty yards from that flat hunk of land is the mountain which rises up into the clouds. The waterfall comes straight down.'

'Is there a trail down from there?' Peters asked.

Slade's eyes flashed across the faces of each of his followers in turn. 'Nope. The only way down from up there is these trails we're looking at. The flat land leads right up to the falls. Ain't no way of riding passed it to get back down. Them falls is so strong they'd crush a horse and rider to mush if'n a man tried to navigate a way down. And most of the gaps down here all lead up to that flat chunk of ground on top. Now do ya see why I'm smiling, boys?'

They all nodded. All except Colby who kept his back to the amused Slade.

'So he's stuck up there?' Colby looked upward. 'Stuck like a raccoon up a tree?'

'Yep. He don't know it yet but he's headed on up into a dead-end, boys. Only way down is the same way he's used to get up there. We got him trapped.'

'If there's boulders this side, what's on the other

side?' Foster asked curiously. 'Maybe he can ride on down over the other side of this rockpile.'

Slade shook his head. His smile grew even wider. 'The only thing on the other side of this hill is a cliff. It's a sheer drop into a lake, Dan. Must be two hundred feet down to that lake. No trail and nothing but flat, sheer rock.'

'So we got him cornered.' Peters grinned.

'Unless he doubles back and comes on down using one of these trails,' Colby suggested, pointing a gloved finger at the many choices before them.

'That ain't gonna happen.' Slade waved at his men. 'Leave ya spare horses here. I want each of ya to take a different trail up through these boulders, boys. There's enough of us to cover almost all of 'em. He'll not get back down this way. Right?'

They all grunted in agreement.

'Fill ya canteens, men,' Colby said as he lowered his own into the river and held on to its leathers. 'Dan? You secure these spare nags to some brush so they don't go wandering when we're up there.'

Foster did as ordered.

Hyram Slade looked at Colby. The gunfighter had never seen a man look so fired-up before by the prospect of killing. It was the look of a man about to go hunting who didn't really require fresh game but simply wanted the thrill of the kill. It was the killing that men like Slade desired. The taste of fresh blood.

As Foster threw himself back on to his horse, Slade tapped his spurs into his mount's flanks and started towards the nearest of the dark trails. He gestured to the others to head on up into the other gaps between the gigantic rocks. The cowboys fanned out as instructed. Each of them took a different route into the maze of trails set in the great wall.

Slade waved a fist in the air. 'See ya all at the top, boys. Remember. We got us a stinking raccoon to kill.'

FOUR

What faced drifter Steve Hardie as he led his worn-out mount to the very top of the long climb was exactly as crazed rancher Hyram Slade, had described it. Emerging from the shadows the exhausted Hardie felt the heat of the ferocious sun find him again. His damp shirt suddenly began to dry and stick to his skin as though it had been glued to his flesh. Hardie was as weary as his lathered-up horse. He reached level ground and fell to his knees. Then he stared straight ahead. For the previous ten minutes he had heard a noise which had reverberated loudly in the confines of the narrow trail. It had sounded like a thunderstorm but there was no thunder nor a storm. Now his eyes told him what had made that deafening noise.

The waterfall was thundering down directly ahead of the flat strip of ground he knelt upon. It roared with all the vigour of nature's most powerful creatures, but this was no wild animal before him. This was something far more dangerous, he thought.

This was raw nature.

Hardie released his grip on the reins and struggled back on to his feet. He was tired, but there was no way he was ever going to allow himself to rest. Not until this nightmare or he himself was finished.

He swayed on legs which felt drained. His feet hurt inside his boots. They felt wet. It was either sweat or blood which now soaked his socks but he knew it was no time to investigate his feet. He staggered forward, leaving his horse to graze on the well-watered blanket of sweet grass and wild flowers. All the drifter could think about was a way of escaping.

Each step was agony. Glass could not have hurt his feet more as he ventured closer and closer to the raging torrent of millions of gallons of water. He felt the fine mist of the spray come over him. It felt good. It seemed to be the only antidote to the merciless rays of the sun high overhead. But where was the trail down from this perilous place?

Somehow Hardie managed to walk as close as he dared to the edge of where the powerful waterfall smashed into the flat strip of land before continuing on its way down into the abyss far below. He looked to his left and felt his heart sinking as though trapped in quicksand.

He paused.

Hardie leaned out slightly and looked down. He then realized that he was on the precipice of a cliff. A high cliff. Caution made him take a step backward as he sensed the wet grass under his boots. He could not see where the constant flow of water ended up far below. Clouds of mist filled the distance between his eyes and the bottom of the sheer drop. He gulped fearfully and looked out. A lake with water as clear as a polished mirror reflected everything down there. Then he saw a river far beyond twisting its way through the trees out into a valley. There were so many trees down there of so many colours he could not make out anything else.

Suddenly Hardie felt his his left boot slip slightly. For a moment he thought that he was falling. He fell backwards and grabbed at the grass to either side of him as his boot kicked some stones over the edge of the high cliff-top.

He did not hear them hit the lake below his high perch. The thunderous roaring of the waterfall drowned out all other sounds. Hardie swallowed hard. He knew that he had come close to following those stones over the top of the cliff and taking what he believed would have been a death fall.

The tired drifter crawled back away from the damp edge of the strip of green ground. His eyes looked at the waterfall and then tried again to see if he might discern a route down.

There was none.

He staggered up on to his feet once more. The boulders behind his grazing horse showed the many trails between their gigantic forms. He went back to his horse and rested a hand upon its saddle.

His eyes were searching.

Searching desperately for another way down from where he found himself, but again it was a fruitless exercise. The drifter was standing upon a strip of fertile ground which led nowhere.

Hardie thought about the rifles of the men who had been chasing him for more than half a day. They had fallen silent hours back.

Why?

Then he nodded to himself.

Of course the Winchesters had fallen silent, he thought. How could they keep shooting at a target they could no longer see? Hardie rubbed his damp face and then tried to dry it with the tails of his bandanna.

'How can I get down from up here?'

The grazing animal continued to ignore its master. Hardie swung on his heels, leaned on the saddle and studied each of the trails to this place in turn. There were a dozen or more apart from the one he had taken. The only way down was to take one of them, he told himself.

'What if they're on their way up here?' he muttered. 'I'm trapped if they are. No place to go.'

He was frightened. He had never looked for a fight and had no stomach for one now. Yet he was cornered and if his pursuers were still coming after him he knew that there was only one way he could survive and that was to kill again.

Kill them all.

The thought sickened him.

The young drifter used his gloves to rub the lather off his horse. The animal kept on eating the grass and flowers that were growing all around them. There had to be another way, his brain kept screaming at him. Another way apart from killing.

Even though his pursuers seemed to want nothing more than to destroy him, Hardie felt sick at the thought of using his guns again. Cripple Creek once more filled his tired mind.

Why had he gone there?

What unknown force had led him to that town of all the places he might have drifted to? He shook his head and rested against the animal who had served him well to have managed to keep them ahead of the lethal lead which had been targeting them since sunup.

Why had that cowboy opened up on him and the sheriff?

It was loco.

The cowboys all acted as though they were above the law.

Hardie paused.

That was it. They acted as though they were above the law because they were above the law, he told himself. Why else would one of their number open up with his hogleg? That cowpoke didn't care if there was a sheriff in the line of fire, he just kept on shooting. Why would anybody do that? Only someone who knew that he was above the law would dare.

Then the words of warning from the lawman returned.

'Get out of here, boy. Ya shouldn't have killed a cowboy.'

Hardie thought about the men who had been trying to kill him all day. Cowboys? Or men who just pretended to be cowboys? There was something going on around the vast range which the drifter had no knowledge of. Why had that sheriff been so afraid? He was a sheriff but Hardie knew there were many kinds of men who wore a tin star in the West. Some were genuine whilst the others were simply token lawmen.

Men paid to give towns the appearance of being law abiding when in truth they were as lawless as they had always been.

Hardie looked at the gaps between the rocks again. The hair on the back of his neck stood on end. He could hear them. The sound of snorting horses responding to spurs challenged the roaring of the waterfall. Their riders' yells filled his ears.

They were coming. They were still coming. Why wouldn't they quit? Why wouldn't they damn well quit? What madness was driving them on?

'Damn it all.' Hardie snatched at his reins and raised his hand. He feverishly clutched the saddle horn and then stepped into his stirrup. Hardie mounted in one swift well practised motion. He poked his right boot into the other stirrup and then looked all around him. He hauled the black gelding's head up. There was nowhere to go, his mind yelled out inside his skull.

The horse turned full circle.

As Hardie held his mount in check he looked to the cascading waterfall. No way to ride down there, he told himself. Then his eyes darted to the cliff edge. He bit his lip. That was a sure way to die, he thought. One last choice remained. He levelled the horse at the boulders.

He swallowed hard.

The drifter knew that if he spurred he would surely ride straight into their rifle barrels. He clutched the reins tightly and steadied the skittish creature beneath him. The gelded black sensed that trouble was close. It began to fight against the bit as its master desperately tried to think.

'Easy, boy,' Hardie said, staring at each of the black trails in turn. So many trails. Which one? Which one?

Then the sound of the horsemen grew louder.

The drifter watched in horror as riders appeared from almost every one of the breaches in the rounded rocks. The bright sunlight danced off the barrels of their rifles as each of the riders dragged their weaponry from their saddle scabbards. The noise of the rifles' mechanisms being cocked filled the strip of land.

Then gunsmoke spewed like the poison from a sidewinder's fangs towards the startled drifter. Plumes of deadly lightning raced from the barrels of the repeating rifles of Slade and his cohorts. Within a heartbeat the air all around the high strip of ground was tainted by shafts of lethal lead. Each bullet was aimed at the trapped drifter. Hardie had no time to draw either of his own weapons as he fought with the startled animal beneath him. The black horse reared up as lead hit it. Blood sprayed across the small clearing. The grass was painted crimson.

The drifter tried to free his boots from the stirrups but the horse kept on rising and clawing at the air as even more bullets cut into its body. No volley of thunderclaps could have equalled the deafening noise of hammers striking rifle bullets and the resulting explosions which erupted from every barrel. Hardie was nearly hit off his saddle as one of the riflemen's shots found its chosen mark. His right hand clutched at his side as the gelding under him buckled and gave out the most pitiful of sounds.

They were tumbling backwards. The drifter clung on to his reins with one hand as the fountains of blood expelled from the bullet-riddled horse. The creature went down, then scrambled defiantly back up but now it was unsteady upon its legs: legs that no longer obeyed its will.

Another series of bullets tore across the distance between Hardie and the cold-hearted riders. He ducked and felt the burning heat of their lead pass just above him as he held his mount's head up to use as a shield. Hardie was soaked in scarlet gore and some of it was his own.

The horse stumbled, staggered and then slid to the edge of the high precipice. The wet ground sloped slightly towards the cliff. Hardie felt the heat from more bullets as they cut through the air all around him. Then there was no more grass beneath the hoofs of his heavy mount. Both horse and its master went over the cliff edge.

The drifter realized he was helpless. His boots were trapped in the stirrups as they both plunged downwards. They were plummeting towards the clouds of vapour at an incredible rate. Hardie vainly attempted to fight himself free of the horse.

Then he saw the water.

It was too late.

FIVE

They say that the Devil has many forms. One was that of the ruthless rancher who sucked in the acrid taste of gunsmoke as he lowered his smoking Winchester. There was no concealing the delight felt by Hyram Slade when his narrowed eyes watched the bloody bullet-ridden horse and its master crash over the rim of the cliff and disappear down into the clouds of rising spray. A million greenbacks could not have made Slade more elated. He gave out a triumphant yell which chilled even the callous souls of those who surrounded him.

'We got the bastard,' Slade blazed. 'I told ya we'd have him trapped up here. See?'

There was no response from any of his men. They had done what he paid them to do but even they felt no satisfaction in their triumph. It had been little more than a turkey shoot. Anyone could get the better of a man who had no chance of going for his guns to reply.

The rancher dismounted faster than any of his hired hands and ran unafraid to the very lip of the grass strip. The desperate hoofs had left a series of deep grooves in the moist turf. Slade's cold calculating eyes burned down as they tried to see the fruits of his labour. He wanted to see a broken body lying on jagged rocks, seeping blood into the otherwise pristine waters of the lake.

Hyram Slade was disappointed.

The clouds of water spray hid what lay directly below his high perch from all prying eyes, especially his. Glee soon turned to indignation as the rest of his men gathered around his broad shoulders. Each man stood holding his rifle in his hands as Slade defied gravity and leaned further over the rim than any of them would have thought possible. What his eyes and soul wanted to see was denied him.

'Where'd he go?' Slade ranted. 'How come I can't see him busted up down there? Why?'

Smoking barrels hot with the frantic expulsion of their magazines' deadly bullets glinted in the sunlight like precious jewels as the men remained a safe distance from the edge of the sheer drop. Unlike their leader, they did not wish to risk following the drifter over that churned-up chunk of sod.

Slade frantically rubbed his neck and growled before turning.

'I can't see him,' the rancher snarled.

None of the others stood within spitting distance of where Slade hovered. He turned and peered down again, his eyes still searching for a hint of his handiwork far below.

The men moved back. The ground was moist with spray from the falls and blood from their rifles' bullets. They all feared following the drifter over the edge.

Only Slade showed no fear.

Colby cranked the last brass casing from his rifle and rested the long weapon against his shoulder. 'No matter,' he said. 'He's dead.'

'What?' Slade swung around and leapt like a panther at his top gunman. He struck out with his hot rifle barrel and caught Colby across the neck. The gunfighter fell on to one knee. He was stunned. So stunned that he did not even see the boot which followed.

Colby groaned and fell on to the bloody grass. The mark of Slade's right boot was imprinted into the side of his face. Blood trickled from his mouth.

'W. . . what ya do that for, boss?' Colby managed to ask through bloody teeth. 'That *hombre* gotta be dead, ain't he?'

Slade marched back to where their mounts stood close to the boulders. He rammed his rifle into its scabbard, then turned. The men who were following him all froze to the spot. Fear swept through them. The rancher raised his right fist and waved it at all of them in turn.

'So he's dead, is he? How come I can't see no body down there?' Slade screamed at the top of his voice. 'How do I know he's dead? Answer me that. How can we be sure he's dead?'

Colby felt the helping hand of Slim Peters assist him back to his feet. He was groggy and it showed. 'There weren't no call for ya to kick me in the head.'

Slade strode back to where Colby was swaying. He poked a finger into the man's chest. 'Ya lucky my rifle was out of shells, Flint. I was gonna shoot ya.'

'It would take a mighty big slice of miracle pie to live after falling that far though, boss,' Peters said cautiously after plucking Colby's rifle off the ground.

'He ain't dead, Slim,' Slade mumbled angrily. 'Not until I see his lifeless corpse is he dead. Savvy?'

Colby spat a lump of bloody spittle at the ground and nursed his jaw. 'Nobody could survive a fall like that.'

'He was rifle-shot,' Foster chipped in. 'I seen him buckle before that black went sliding.'

'Dan's right.' Peters nodded. 'I seen him hit as well.'

Slade clenched his fist and waved it under Colby's chin. 'I want his head on a pike. I'll place it in the middle of Cripple Creek for all the folks to see. Learn the bastards who's the boss of this country. We gotta go down there and find him. We don't want him crawling off to find himself some real law.'

'How we gonna get from here to all the ways down there?' Foster asked. 'That drifter took the only way down I can figure but there ain't no way any of us is likely to follow him over that cliff, boss.'

Slade turned away from them. 'We go back down the way we got up here and then head west. We have to swing around the mountain of boulders for about twenty miles and then cut back. There's a trail that leads to the lake and on to a little town called Senora.'

'That'll take weeks,' Peters commented. 'His body ain't likely to be there by the time we reach the lake. Critters will have probably picked his bones clean long before then.'

Colby wanted to argue but his head hurt. He spat another mouthful of blood and rubbed his throbbing skull. 'Let's head on down now, boys. Sooner we starts the sooner we gets there.'

'I figure it'll take the best part of a day to get to the lake and another few to ride on to Senora,' Slade opined.

'What's in Senora?' another of the cowboys asked.

'They got a pretty sweet range there,' Slade informed them with an emphatic nod. 'Might be a few hundred head of steers we can rustle.'

'Kill two birds with one stone.' Peters smiled.

'Even if we don't find that drifter's carcass we can do a little business. Right, boss?'

'Damn right,' Slade agreed. 'But we'll find that drifter and if he is still alive we'll finish him.'

The men trailed Slade nervously back to their horses. Each keeping distance between themselves and their leader. They mounted and watched as the rancher held his lines in his gloved hands thoughtfully.

None dared open their mouths.

After a few moments Slade looked at one of his quieter men named simply Cass. 'Cass? You head on back to the ranch and get Smith and Masters and follow us to the lake with their irons. We'll need our best brand-burners if we do happen to stumble on a herd.'

Slim Peters gave a chortle. 'I can almost smell that fur burning, boss.'

Cass swung his sturdy mount and spurred. The small quarter horse sped down into one of the black gaps in the rocks. The beats of its hoofs echoed around the others. The rancher raised a hand.

'C'mon. We got us at least five hours hard riding before sundown.' Slade turned his horse and thrust his spurs backward into the animal's flesh. The horse obeyed.

Like a line of monks on their way to evening prayers the horsemen silently retraced their tracks down through the winding trails towards the river.

Each of the hired gunmen had learned an important lesson. Men were only dead when Hyram Slade said they were dead.

SIX

The water was cold. So very cold. Only ice could have been colder. Scarlet clouds of swirling blood looped like a lasso around the spot where the horse and its master had crashed into the lake. The unconscious drifter had no knowledge of that or anything else. Steve Hardie was only alive because the black gelding had crashed into the lake before him and broken the otherwise deadly impetus of his fall. He had been dragged down to the floor of the lake like a rag doll, leaving a trail of blood in his wake.

His right boot remained trapped in its stirrup, but again the drifter knew nothing about that either. Luckily the brutal impact had knocked him out completely. The drifter and his dead mount kept returning to the surface only to be forced back beneath the water by the inexorable force of the waterfall. There were few things more powerful than a waterfall that refused to quit. The prophetic words of Flint Colby uttered earlier far above the lake were nearly vindicated. Death was only a few heartbeats away for the unconscious Hardie as the last of the precious air left his mouth and he was dragged down once more.

Then a miracle happened.

A miracle which Hardie would never know anything about. The current from the cascading deluge of water as it hit the lake sucked the dead horse up toward the exact spot where it hit the surface. Clouds of white ghostly vapour concealed the exact spot where the horse's body became snared in its powerful fury. Both the horse and the helpless drifter were spun around as though they had been caught in a maelstrom. Trails of crimson spiralled through the foam like the web of a demonic spider.

Around and around the horse was spun beneath the never-ending downfall of water with its master's foot still caught in the sodden stirrup. Hardie's trapped form broke surface several times and although still unconscious he managed to suck air into lungs functioning only through the basic instinct of survival.

Then his foot became dislodged from his boot and he was thrown across the wide expanse of water. Colliding with the bank Hardie briefly regained consciousness and gasped for air. His stunned mind managed to see the unfamiliar setting he found himself in.

Then everything went blank again as he slipped back into the nightmarish depths. The cold water would either protect or kill him. The drifter broke back into the air once more and dimly realized that he was being washed further and further away from where he and his mount had landed. There was something hauling him away from the foot of the falls. Something far stronger than his befuddled brain could understand.

Hardie crashed over a shallow wall of rocks. He was no longer in the lake but somewhere else even more hostile. The fast-moving creek hauled him into its waters and thrust him headlong down its winding turbulence. Its rocks tore at his clothing and flesh as he was swept helplessly along. His arms reached out and his fingers tried to grab at anything which might slow or even stop his journey. But his numbed fingers did not obey. His bruised mind vainly attempted to comprehend what was happening to him but again the drifter found only failure. Then the river beyond the creek claimed him.

He crashed through a muddy wall of reeds and then rolled over until he was swept into the river. His senses told him he was now travelling faster than ever. The surging current was far stronger in the deeper river than it had been in the creek but that was of no consolation. Again the injured man tried to fight his way out of the dangerous flow.

Again he failed.

Hardie could not feel a thing. The nearly ice-cold water had numbed his entire body. He had no sense of anything any longer except the sensation of being propelled by unseen watery power down the deep river.

He pitched over like a sinking Indian canoe, helpless against the current that impelled his dazed and confused body along the river's length. The cold water protected him from new and old pain alike but Hardie was not thankful. He tried to swim but he could not control his arms and legs. The river drove him on. He was helpless. The drifter wanted out of this place, to crawl back on to dry land. Hardie knew only too well that the river could easily become his grave.

Hardie tried to think, to understand, but it was like a drunken memory. The entire world was spinning like a child's wooden top. Or was it just him? Fleeting memories began to come to his mind whenever it managed to claw its way out of the black nightmarish oblivion. Memories of the cliff-top. Of the bullets and the blood. Then the drifter hit tree roots and submerged jagged rocks hidden from view along the length of the fast-moving river.

Yet there was still no pain.

A chilling realization overwhelmed him. He was no longer the master of his own destiny but the helpless victim of whatever fate held in store for him. Somewhere ahead he would discover the truth.

Hardie suddenly felt his entire body being lifted and thrown as though he were departing the back of a wild mustang. He crashed back down and then hit a tree root which was shaped like a horse's back leg. The impact sent Hardie spinning full circle beneath the water. He clawed at the waves around him and was then sent hurtling into the bank of the river with such force that he was knocked senseless.

More dead than alive Hardie hurtled along the waterway colliding with everything in his path. A turn in the course of the mighty river sent him ploughing head first up on to its muddy bank. He lay there on his face like a corpse, with arms outstretched on either side of him as the water tried to drag his lower half back into its black depths.

The burning sun beat down mercilessly across the grassland which fringed the river. A rider had been drawn to cross the range by the earlier echoes of the rifle fire. The weathered horseman dragged his reins to his chest and steadied his handsome stallion. He was only a quarter of a mile away from where Hardie's limp body had been brought to an abrupt stop but the rider knew nothing of that. It was curiosity that had brought him there. Few men ever fired their weaponry around Senora unless there was trouble.

The horseman lowered his reins. He ran a gloved hand along the neck of his chestnut. Tom Steele then stood in his stirrups and squinted at the sunlit river in the distance. His eyes briefly glanced up to the high cliff-top.

'Did ya hear that, boy?' Steele asked the horse as he sat back down. 'Some critters bin doing a lot of shooting. Let's go take us a looksee.'

The rancher leaned forward and spurred. The powerful horse was quick into its stride and raced through the high grass towards the river that cut through Steele's Bar T ranch.

They say that curiosity has killed many a cat but no one ever mentions that sometimes it can help save the hide of a half-drowned drifter sucking in mud.

SEVEN

The big stallion thundered across the range of sweet swaying grass. Its master dug his boots into his stirrups, hung on to his reins and allowed the animal its head. Few other horses could have matched the pace of the chestnut when in full flight. The inquisitive ranch owner reached the river quickly, but found nothing to quench his thirst for answers beneath the verdant canopies of trees in full leaf.

There was no sign of anyone having fired rifles, either at the edge of the range of tall grass or along the muddy ground which fringed the river's length. Tom Steele allowed the animal to trot up and down along the bend in the river on the damp red soil for five minutes before dragging his reins back and halting the creature. Steele glanced back up at the high cliff close to the waterfall and tried to fathom what had occurred only a very few minutes earlier.

Someone had been doing an awful lot of shooting. Rifle-shooting. But who? And why? It was unheard of in these parts and that troubled the rancher.

Sweating in the burning heat of the sun his magnificent stallion pawed a hoof impatiently at the ground. Its master remained astride its broad back, staring upwards. Then Steele's attention was drawn back to what lay ahead of his horse. It was the sound of the fast-flowing water. It filled the air all around them.

Looking down, Steele noticed the deep grooves that his stallion was making in the ground. He patted the animals neck and loosened his grip on the reins which had kept the animal in check.

'Go on then. Get ya belly full of water, boy.' Steele had barely finished his sentence before the stallion began to walk across the mud until it reached the sloping ground which led down to the reed-fringed river.

Steele leaned back as the horse lowered its neck and began to drink. He rested the palm of one hand on the cantle of his saddle and looked all around the raging river. This river had kept his stock alive during all the years that he had lived in these parts. Again his thoughts went to who could have been firing their rifles. Perhaps, he pondered, the sound had carried from far beyond the mountain. He tried to relax.

It was impossible.

Something was gnawing at his innards.

As the stallion drank Steele noticed its ears twitch, as though listening out for danger. At first he was not concerned. He sighed and thought about filling his own canteen, but there seemed little point. He was only ten minutes' ride from his ranch house and there was plenty of water there.

Suddenly the horse lifted its head and stared down the twisting course of the waterway. It snorted as though angry or afraid. The horseman tilted his head and looked to where the animal's attention seemed to be fixed.

'What's wrong, boy?' Steele asked his mount as it began to shift nervously in the water.

Then the rancher squinted hard. To his utter surprise he saw two sodden legs floating just beyond a bush of thorns, under a wide-girthed tree. One foot still had its high-heeled boot attached to it but the other was bare. The light from the sun was filtering down through the leaves of the tree. Golden rays of light danced on the splashing water, which appeared to be trying to haul the owner of the legs into the river. The legs were floating as the powerful current swirled and sucked along the river's course.

'What we got there? A body?' Steele gathered up his reins, turned the head of the stallion and tapped his spurs. The tall horse walked along the muddy bank towards the pair of feet. The stallion was anxious. Fearful. It continued to snort its disapproval and fight with its master. Water slashed up over them both as the horse raised its forelegs, shying in protest.

The rancher had seen a good many dead things in his fifty-one years of existence and was ready to look at one more. He reined in his nervous mount and looked down at Steve Hardie's unmoving form. The body was bloody from head to toe. His clothing had been torn by the rocks upriver. No whipping could have matched nature's handling of the helpless drifter. Whoever this man was he had sure taken a beating, Steele surmised.

'Easy, boy,' Steele said firmly to his skittish mount. The horse was not easily pacified. It sensed death or something close to that final state and wanted to run. Every instinct in the wide-eyed horse wanted to put as much distance between itself and Hardie as possible. It took all of the rancher's strength to keep the stallion from bolting. 'Damn it all. Easy. Ain't nothing to be feared about. Easy, ya silly old fool. Sometimes I reckon ya more filly than stallion.'

All the words were wasted. The stallion wanted nothing to do with what it sensed was a carcass.

Gripping the reins with gloved fists, Steele steered the horse further along and then spurred up the embankment before attempting to dismount. He looked at the head and shoulders of the drifter. There seemed to be no sign of life but Steele knew he had to make sure. He knew that it never paid to bury a man unless you were real certain the poor critter was dead.

The rancher raised his right leg, swung it out over his saddle and dropped to the muddy ground. His hands reached out, grabbed a low-hanging branch from the tree and began to tie his reins to it. Every movement was accompanied by soft words designed to calm his horse.

He had barely released his grip on the leather lines, when the stallion reared up and ripped the branch from the trunk of the tree. Steele reached out but the frightened animal had turned and thundered out into the long, swaying grass. The rancher slapped his chaps with both hands and vainly bellowed after the fleeing stallion. The horse had made up its mind. The only place it was going to stop was back in its stable.

'Damn it all,' Steele cursed shaking his head. 'I knew I should have had that bastard gelded. That's too much horse for an old man.'

A flustered Steele sighed heavily and turned. His experienced eyes looked down at the body lying a couple of feet from his pointed boot-tips.

'Reckon I'd better check ya over, young 'un. Seems hardly worth the knee-ache but a man deserves to be treated right even if he is buzzard bait.' Steele took a step back down into the soft mud and knelt beside the drifter's shoulders. His gloved hands were of little use in checking out flesh. The rancher removed the gloves and rammed them into his jacket pockets. His fingers rested on the neck of the cold man. He could feel no pulse. 'Damn. Ya real cold, boy.'

His fingers moved over the cuts and bruises revealed by the shredded shirt. Then they came across the graze along Hardie's ribs.

'Rifle shot,' Steele declared knowingly. 'So it was *you* them Winchesters were firing at. I wonder what ya done to attract so much lead.'

The body had been washed of all its natural colour by the icy water. Hardie was pale, as pale as most dead men ever get. Steele's strong hands gripped Hardie's right shoulder and pulled it over until the man's face was revealed. Mud covered almost every part of the drifter's front. Steele pulled his bandanna free and leaned over to soak it in the river water. He began to clean the mud off Hardie's face.

Then, as he rinsed the bandanna in the cold water, Steele heard a sound in the chest of the apparantly dead man lying at his knees. His eyes widened.

'Death rattles,' Steele muttered to himself. 'I done heard about them.'

Not for the first time in his life Tom Steele found himself proved wrong. Suddenly Hardie shook and then coughed. Water flooded out from the corners of his mouth as his fingers clenched and clawed like talons at the mud to either side of him.

Steele dropped the bandanna. It was washed away swiftly but the stunned rancher did not notice. His unblinking eyes and open mouth were aimed at the body beside him. A body which somehow was still alive.

Hardie's hand grabbed the nearer of Steele's wrists. For a dead man the grip was pretty powerful.

'Who are ya?' Steele managed to utter.

The drifter coughed out more of the river water, then jolted up on to one elbow. His glazed eyes blinked hard, then they locked on to the rancher.

'I'm alive?' Hardie gasped in utter amazement.

'Yeah and ya frightened the hell out of me.' Steele retorted.

The confused Hardie coughed again. More water spewed out on to the mud as the drifter felt his heart starting to pound inside his chest. He rubbed the filth from his lips and forced himself to sit up. His hands checked his guns. They were still holstered and held in place by the safety loops around their hammers.

'Where am I?' Hardie asked, feeling his side start to hurt as though a branding-iron had been thrust into him. Both men looked at the graze. Blood began to trickle from the gash.

'Ya on the Bar T, son,' Steele said as he managed to get back to his feet. 'Where'd ya figure ya was?'

The drifter rubbed his face. He did not answer.

He remembered the shooting and the fall. Everything else was a blurred nightmare.

Steele held out a hand and helped the unsteady man to his feet. 'Ya lost a boot there, sonny.'

Hardie nodded and looked back. 'I lost me a lot more than a boot, friend. I did have me a damn good black gelding.'

'Ya lost a whole horse?' Steele shook his head.

'Not exactly, pard,' Hardie corrected. 'The poor critter was shot out from under me.'

'Who by?' The rancher was inquisitive.

'Damned if I know.' The drifter walked out into the sunlight. The heat felt good on his exposed skin.

Then both men heard the unmistakable sound of horses approaching at speed. They turned quickly on their heels and looked out across the tall grass. The nervous drifter raised himself up to his full height and stared hard.

Hardie's hands instinctively rested on the grips of his holstered Colts. His thumbs stayed ready to flick off the leather safety loops from their hammers.

'Easy, son,' Steele said, calmly touching the sleeve of the drifter. 'Ain't no call to be alarmed. That's just my daughter bringing my damn horse back.'

The drifter remained alert and alarmed until he saw the face of Kate Steele for himself. Then his arms lowered down to his torn pants as he gazed silently up at her. The fiesty female was small. She was also beautiful for someone clad in cut-down cowboy gear. Her blonde hair floated out from under her wide-brimmed hat and reached her narrow shoulders. She expertly dragged her reins back and seemed almost to be standing on her saddle as her grey pony came to a halt. She had the reins of her father's stallion tied securely to her saddle horn.

'What ya doing giving me a scare like. . . .' Kate Steel's words faded as she saw the young man bathed in the bright afternoon sun.

'Kate.' Her father smiled up at her.

She did not notice. All Kate Steele could see was the handsome drifter standing in his ripped trail clothes less than five feet from the nose of her mount.

Steele rubbed his whiskered chin and looked at the daughter and then at the tall stranger. A smile spread across his rugged features as he recalled his own lost youth. He knew it was pointless talking to either of them. Neither would hear a word. All he and the girl would do was stare open-mouthed at one another.

The rancher guided the drifter to his stallion and urged him to mount. Without taking his eyes from the female for even a second Hardie mounted the rancher's sturdy horse. Tom Steele lifted his leg and poked his boot into the stirrup before hauling himself up behind the drifter.

They headed towards the distant ranch house.

EIGHT

A silence seemed to have settled over the small ranch house and its outbuildings set in the centre of the vast range. Not even the sound of the powerful falls was reaching the wooden buildings. Tom Steele had noticed it long before his daughter or their guest had ventured out into the late afternoon sun as the fiery orb sank to the far horizon. The range had a way of getting into a person's bones. It spoke to them. Only those who lived their lives upon its vastness truly understood its mystery. When it hurt, they felt its pain. There was something wrong out there and the old rancher felt it in every sinew of his weathered body.

Steele sucked on the stem of his corncob pipe and rocked in his favourite chair on the veranda. He did not mention his concerns to the young pair. His wrinkled eyes studied all that lay before him. He glanced up at the quiet twosome who stood over him and again smiled to himself. The drifter now sported a new pair of pants and a clean shirt to replace the trail gear which had been shredded in the violent waters of the river.

Steele ran a match along his pants leg, touched the bowl of his pipe and made smoke. He had tried to assist his daughter in tending the wounds of the young man, but had been shushed away. Kate had wanted Hardie for herself and Kate always got what she wanted.

In the three or so hours that Steve Hardie had been at the ranch Tom Steele had not learned anything about the young man with the handsome holstered shooting-rig. Each of his questions had been ambushed by his daughter, who wanted to discover more about the man who had seemed to have fallen like an angel into their lives.

Her questions were not like those vainly posed by her father. Kate had wanted to know whether the drifter was married. Had he a sweetheart somewhere awaiting his return? She sought the sort of vital information only single females ever asked of a potential mate. It amused the older man that they stood so close to one another that it would be hard to get a cigarette paper between them, and yet neither of them knew what to do next. Both yearned for the other but were afraid. Steele had travelled that road himself a long time ago when he had first met Kate's mother. His eyes travelled to the small white picket-fence close to the barn and the well-tended plot of flowers which encircled a small marker. It had been a long time since he had buried his wife there, yet it seemed like only yesterday that he had first encountered her.

'Enjoy ya vittles?' Steele asked through a cloud of pipe smoke. 'Kate's a mighty fine hand with a skillet. Her mother, God rest her soul, was even better.'

The fading light of the setting sun did not hide the blushes which lit up Kate's beautiful face. She turned and leaned on the porch upright. 'Hush up, Pa. It was only eggs and beans.'

'It was the best meal I've had in years, sir,' Hardie said in a low drawl as he noticed her glance at him. They both averted their eyes.

Steele nodded and rocked. 'Ya looking for work?'

'Yep,' Hardie answered.

Kate turned and scolded her father. 'Can't ya wait for his grub to settle before ya go trying to hire him, Pa? He's bin hurt, ya know.'

'Sit down, boy.' The older man patted a bench set close to the rocking-chair and watched as Hardie sat down. It was obvious the youngster was hurting. Nobody could navigate the creek or the river without ending up in a lot of pain. 'I figure that ya have to earn some money after losing all ya goods with that horse of yours. We can't afford to pay much but I never cheat a man who does an honest day's work. I'll give ya a horse and Kate'll make sure ya gets to eat ya fill. What ya say?'

Kate did not waste a heartbeat. As soon as the drifter had seated himself she moved next to him ensuring her leg touched his.

Hardie swallowed hard. His eyes moved between both the Steele family members in turn. 'Thank ya kindly, sir. I'll work mighty hard for ya.'

Kate stroked Hardie's hand without even realizing she was doing it. 'Ya don't have to work too hard, Steve. Not until ya feeling better.'

Steele's eyes had seen his daughter's stroking. 'My name's Tom, boy. Ya call me Tom.'

Hardie nodded. 'That I will, Tom. Ya both bin awful kind to me and I won't let either of ya down.'

The older man held the pipe stem in his teeth and looked at his lovesick daughter. 'Go put the coffee on, Kate. Steve here looks darn thirsty.'

Kate jumped back to her feet. 'Sure, Pa. I'll put the coffee on right now.'

Both men watched her rush back into the ranch house. Hardie looked embarrassed. Steele smiled at the drifter.

'She kinda likes ya, boy. Likes ya a lot.'

'I'd noticed,' Hardie whispered back.

'She ain't never cottoned to a man before,' Steele said. 'Not in a real grown-up way. I see a lot of her mother in her right about now.'

The drifter looked over his shoulder. 'She sure is mighty pretty, Tom.'

'If ya hurts her, I'll surely kill ya,' Steele added. 'Big as ya are I'll not let anyone hurt my Kate. Understand?'

'I couldn't hurt her, Tom.' Hardie sighed heavily. 'She's the most wonderful gal I ever met.'

'Good, boy.' Steele gave the scene another knowing look. The sun had disappeared now and the sky was red. 'Something's wrong out there. It's too damn quiet. Ain't a peep coming from my steers. They sense it as well.'

Hardie leaned forward and looked at the swaying grass as the light slowly faded. 'Might be them varmints who bin chasing me for the longest while, Tom. Maybe they've followed me into the valley.'

Steele tapped the ash from his pipe and rose. The drifter rose too, and went to stand beside the rancher.

'Kate's real taken with ya, Steve. But I got me a feeling that ya might be right. Them back-shooting *hombres* could be still on ya trail. If they brings trouble here. . . .

Hardie rested his hand on the older man's shoulder. 'I might be a tad beat up, Tom, but I'll protect you and Kate with my life. I owes ya both.'

Tom Steele looked up into the face of the drifter. 'Ya any good with them guns?'

Hardie gave a slow nod. 'Yep.'

'That's fine, boy. Real fine.'

*

The settlement of Senora was small and quiet by the usual yardsticks. It was a town which, against all the odds, survived. It was a place where nothing ever changed. It had a saloon and a doctor who made more money tending horses and steers than he had ever made treating people. It had a sheriff who had grown old vainly waiting for something to happen. A feed store and a barber shop and little else occupied the single street which made up the whole place. That was Senora. A place which lived off the produce of the ranchers who grazed their stock on the fertile range.

Fewer than a hundred people lived in the small town and everyone knew everyone else. They had never wanted Senora to become like other towns, to grow and become prosperous. They were content. The ranchers and their families and their cowboys were the same. In its entire history Senora had never had any trouble.

None of them expected that to change. No one ever imagined that trouble would find their quiet community and deliver its venomous fury. Bad things happened in other places to other folks. Not to them.

The people of Senora were to be proved wrong.

Trouble came in many forms. One of those forms were creatures who lived their own lives by the gun. Creatures who shied away from hard work, to steal and kill whenever they desired to do so. Sick two-legged men who were unworthy of being called men in its purest sense. Those men trailed Hyram Slade into the cool valley towards the lake set at the foot of the mighty waterfall. The bright moon overhead gave no clue to the danger the dozen or more riders posed.

Nightfall covered the undergrowth in its blanket of darkness as Slade drew his leathers up and stopped his horse close to the edge of the lake. The sound of the falling water as it kept on crashing into the lake's wide expanse of rippling water did not ease up just because the sun had given way to the large moon.

It was like the noise of a locomotive hitting a full head of steam. Yet Slade did not hear it. His mind was wholly focused on finding the body of the drifter who had killed one of his worthless followers, a creature who, like all the other riders around him, proclaimed himself to be a cowboy. Yet no real cowboy did what Slade and his men did. Few of them ever killed without a single thought for their victims. In fact, few real cowboys even carried a gun as they went about their daily rituals.

That was what made Slade and his men different. Each of them was armed to the teeth with every conceivable weapon.

No troop of cavalrymen could have been better equipped than those who rode for Slade.

The half-crazed horseman dropped to the

ground and walked as far as it was possible to walk without sinking into the black waters of the lake.

'We'll wait until Ty and Huck get here with Cass,' Slade announced before turning. 'Make a fire and rustle up some grub.'

Colby dismounted, looped his reins around a tree stump and tightened the leathers. 'We gonna rustle us some steers before sunup, boss?'

'Yep,' Slade answered.

Colby watched the others speedily preparing a place to start piling kindling. His eyes then returned to the man who had nearly broken his jaw hours earlier. 'Ya sure there are steers out there, boss?'

'Damn right I'm sure.' Slade moved away from the water. His eyes squinted out from the trees and brush to where the range beckoned. 'See 'em? See them longhorns catching the moonlight, Flint?'

The gunfighter looked hard. 'I reckon.'

'I count at least a hundred. All waiting for us to adopt them and take them to a better place.' Slade was laughing. It was his usual sick laughter, which frightened all those who stood around him.

Colby clapped his hands together at the others. 'Git that fire lit up. I'm powerful hungry.'

Slade rubbed his jaw. 'I hear tell that Senora got itself a sheriff that's so old he oughta be dead. Sounds like a place we should visit after we've eaten.'

Dan Foster dropped an armful of kindling on to

the ground and searched his pockets for a match. 'Why would we wanna head to a two-bit town like that for, boss?'

Hyram Slade's lips curled like those of a rabid hound. He began to chuckle to himself. 'To take it for everything it's got, Dan.'

They all wanted to ask why. None had the courage to do so.

NINE

There was an urgency in the whipping leathers as they forced their mounts away from the roaring campfire and on to the sleepy, unsuspecting town downriver. The horsemen rode at a fast pace along the length of the winding waterway which stretched all the way to Senora and beyond. They had filled their unworthy innards with salt pork and beans and were ready for the bloody night's work.

The madness which had haunted Hyram Slade for as long as he had lived was now leading his riders on to yet another pitiful conquest. A conquest of the strong over the innocent. Slade drove his spurs into the flanks of the powerful animal beneath him and drove on. Now all the so-called rancher had in his mind was killing. He had failed to discover the body of the drifter and prove to himself he and his hired guns had dispatched another upstart into the whirlpools of death. Now his attention was diverted to other potential victims of his wrath. His craving for the sight and taste of fresh blood had to be satisfied. Satisfied by killing anything which stood between him and his appetite for even more wealth and the additional power it would bring.

There were sixteen of them now. Sixteen hardened killers all riding with one purpose. They knew the town of Senora was a place where they would find easy pickings. It had the reputation of being a peaceful settlement. That would be its downfall. To Slade the word peaceful meant only one thing. It meant they would find little or no resistance to the arsenal of guns they all carried and were eager to use again.

Death was the only certain way to ensure there would never be any witnesses to what they had planned. If they had to murder every man, woman and child within the unmarked boundaries of Senora, that was what they would willingly do.

The further along the river the horsemen rode the more steers they saw grazing on the lush pasture. The range spread out like a blanket for as far as the moonlight would allow them to see. Tall grass filled that range and the bellies of the cattle which grazed its seemingly limitless acreage. Yet in truth Slade did not need or even want those steers. He had far more than most honest men ever managed to accumulate. What he really wanted was to punish everyone not in his employ.

To relish the kill.

They say that once a sane man has tasted blood it creates an appetite within him which eventually devours his soul. Like opium it becomes a drug which has to be repeatedly experienced. When a man has a brain that has become poisoned to the point of madness, the results are even worse.

The town's lights were few but enough to give the savage group of rustlers a target at which to aim their lathered-up mounts. They all knew that was their goal. Their chosen place. Like moths to a naked flame they all spurred on and on. They would kill before midnight. Again they would do their vicious leader's dirty work with no hint of remorse. To feel remorse a man had to have a conscience and none of those who followed the dust of the crazed Slade had anything inside him but the blackened beating of a killer's heart. Men who lived the way every one of Slade's henchmen did never thought of anything except their next payday.

Bathed in moonlight the riders ploughed on.

Once they had destroyed the small unsuspecting town, they would turn their attention to the cattle which Slade had already decided were his to take.

The brand-burners had brought all their irons with them and had left them heating up in the camp-fire close to the lake. By the time they returned the irons would be ready to alter the brands of every single steer that they had rounded up.

There was a fortune out there, Slade told himself. He had first thought that there might be a hundred head of longhorns hidden by the tall grass of the range. Now as he got closer to Senora he realized that there could be ten times that number, out there. The unearthly light of the moon danced among the cattle's horns. So many beeves were there that Slade began to convince himself that what he intended doing was almost a holy crusade. This would not be just brutal murder and common cattle-rustling. A soiled brain could justify anything. Slade's had already forgiven him.

The lights from distant ranch houses dotted around the vast range sparkled like jewels, but that was of no concern to any of the merciless riders. By the time any of the ranchers out there heard the shots of the slaughter Slade had planned for the people of the tiny town, it would be too late.

Too damn late.

Yet there was one ranch house much closer to the town than any of its neighbours, and that was where the tall drifter stood beside Tom Steele, blowing the steam off the top of his coffee cup.

Steve Hardie lowered the cup from his lips and took a step closer to the edge of the veranda. He straightened his aching body up to its full height and lowered his chin. His keen, youthful eyes were a lot sharper than those of the man he stood beside.

'What's eatin' ya, son?' Steele wondered.

'Do ya have any hands out there, Tom?' Hardie questioned pointing a finger towards the area of the lake.

'I ain't got me no hands exceptin' you, Steve,' Steele answered. 'Why?'

'I see me a fire,' the drifter replied. 'A well-fed campfire by the looks of it.'

Steele screwed up his entire face as his older eyes tried to see what the youngster was pointing at. 'Oh yeah. I see it. Now who on earth would be out there at this hour?'

The beautiful female walked out to join the two men. Hardie glanced at her and then back to the flames licking up into the dark star-filled sky a few miles away. 'Can ya see a fire out there, Kate?'

She gave a fleeting look. 'Yep.'

'Ya do?' Tom Steele looked troubled. He finished his coffee and handed the cup to his daughter with a grateful nod. The rancher stepped closer to the tall drifter. 'What else them eagle eyes of yours see, Steve boy?'

Hardie felt a cold chill trace his spine beneath the new shirt he wore. He swallowed hard. The aim of his finger changed direction as he pointed towards the river and the line of trees which flanked it. The light from the moon and stars made it impossible for the horsemen to hide.

'I see me a whole heap of riders.'

Steele felt his face twitch. 'Damn it all. I can see

92

them as well. Must be twenty of the varmints.'

'Any of the other ranchers got themselves a bunch of cowboys as big as that?' Hardie asked.

Tom Steele cleared his throat and shook his head of white hair. 'Nope. I don't reckon there's that many cowboys on this whole range, son.'

Hardie placed his cup down and ran fingers through his dark hair thoughtfully. 'Then that has to be the men who was chasing and trying to kill me. Damn it all. Why won't they quit, Tom? It's plumb loco not to quit, ain't it?'

'Who are they?' Kate ventured curiously. 'What men are ya talking about, Steve?'

'Wish I knew,' Hardie replied. 'All I know about them is that they tried their best to finish me off.'

Kate gasped. 'Oh Lord!'

'Maybe they're headed to Senora to ask if anyone seen a stranger,' Steele suggested. 'Lucky for you we came here and didn't go to town.'

Hardie rested his hands on the wooden veranda rail. He kept watching the riders lit up by the eerie blue moonlight. They were riding fast and furious. The moonlight caught the rifles some of Slade's men were holding.

'I don't reckon their sort ask a lot of questions, Tom,' he said. 'I reckon they've got something else planned. Something a lot worse than any of us could imagine.'

'Like what?' Kate asked.

Hardie sighed. 'Killing, Kate. Them varmints sure tried to kill me for the longest while. I don't see anyone is safe when they get their repeating rifles out. The folks in Senora gotta be warned so they can protect themselves just in case.'

'There ain't many guns in Senora, boy,' Steele said in a dry, disquieted tone. 'If that bunch are bent on shooting, they could slaughter the whole town in the blink of an eye.'

The drifter nodded. 'I gotta go there.'

'We gotta go there,' Steele corrected.

The anxious female rushed to the arm of the brooding young man and clung to it. 'No. They might kill ya, Steve. If'n it's killing they want to do, ya ain't safe.'

'None of the folks in Senora are safe either,' Hardie observed as he checked his guns. 'At least I got me a pair of .45s and I know how to use them.'

Steele looked to the horsemen and then at the lights of the small settlement. 'A man might be able to beat them to town on a fast horse.'

'Lend me that stallion of yours, Tom?' the drifter asked the older man.

'He's a real handful,' Steele warned.

'Never met a stallion that weren't, Tom.' Hardie nodded. 'As long as he's fast, I'll hang on.'

'No.' Kate was almost weeping. 'Ya survived their guns once, Steve. Don't give them a chance to finish what they started.'

94

'I'll get the ornery critter saddled up.' Steele stepped down from the veranda and headed towards the barn. 'I'll saddle the buckskin for myself. I got me a scattergun just itching to let some buckshot rip.'

Kate turned to the drifter and looked up into his face. He could feel her body pressed into his. It was warm and soft. Her heart was pounding and Hardie felt every beat.

'It's suicide,' she said.

'Maybe' he drawled.

'There are too many of them.' Tears filled her eyes. 'I've waited all my life to meet someone like you. Ya can't go. I can't let ya go, Steve.'

'Ya might be right about them killing me,' Hardie said. 'I sure hope ya ain't.'

Kate reached up and dragged his head down. Her lips found his and she worked them hard. Without even realizing it, his hands wrapped around her dainty form and lifted her up. He cradled her there until she pulled her mouth away from his.

'Stay here,' she begged.

'I can't,' he said.

'Why not?'

'I ain't too sure.' Hardie sighed as he savoured the taste of her lips. 'All I know is that I have to go and see what's happening. If those are the varmints who tried to kill me, I led them here. It'll be my fault if anyone gets hurt in Senora. And by my reckoning, I'm the only one who can stop it.'

'Ya're still beat up.' She sighed sorrowfully.

'I'm OK,' he insisted.

It was a panting Steele who came running out of the barn with the stallion in tow. Hardie lowered Kate until her feet touched the boards once more. He released his grip on the beautiful female and caught the reins from the rancher.

Steele turned and started to hurry back to the barn. 'Wait for me, boy. I gotta saddle my old buckskin and get my gun.'

Hardie checked his holstered Colts. They had dried out since he had cleared the river. He touched Kate's chin and gave her a kiss on her temple.

'I'll return,' he promised.

For a moment Kate could not speak. It felt as though a noose had been tightened around her throat, strangling everything she wanted to say. Her small hands touched his arms until his eyes found hers again.

'I promise,' he whispered.

She nodded.

The drifter kissed her, turned and jumped on to the back of the skittish stallion. The animal reared up but Hardie held it in check until its fore hoofs returned to the ground. The chestnut snorted.

Kate reached out. 'They might kill ya.'

Steve Hardie smiled. 'They'll surely try but I take an awful lot of killing, Kate. Tell ya pa to round up the other ranchers and meet me in town. I might need all the help I can muster.'

Before she could say another word Hardie had swung the horse's head round and spurred the powerful stallion into action. It thundered away towards the distant town, leaving only dust hanging on the lantern-lit air.

Kate wanted to scream. Then her attention was drawn to the large open doors of the barn. Her father came out of the huge wooden structure, leading his buckskin. He had heard the sound of the stallion's hoofs pounding away from the ranch courtyard. He glanced at his daughter in disbelief.

'That young fool. I told him to wait.'

Kate rubbed the tears from her eyes on her shirtsleeve and came down to where her father stood. 'He said for ya to round up the other ranchers, Pa.'

Steele ran into the house. When he reappeared he was holding his scattergun and a box of cartridges. 'Get ya pony saddled, girl. I'm going after Steve before he gets himself killed. You go round up the other ranchers and bring them to town. Hear me?'

'I hear ya, Pa.' Kate watched her father mount his buckskin and ride after the drifter. She rushed into the barn for her pony. The beautiful female had never been so afraid before. She thought of Steve Hardie's words.

Kate prayed that the handsome stranger would be able to keep his promise and return to her.

TEN

Lawman Will Holt had been the sheriff of Senora long before his bones had started to lock up as time took its toll on his aged body. Summer had become winter yet the old-timer had never considered retiring from the job he loved. Apart from the occasional brawl his time in Senora had been mainly uneventful. Holt had grown old and the tin star he proudly wore had rusted like his joints but it did not matter to him. He was content with his lot and did not fear what the future might hold for him. He had long known that unlike most towns Senora did not really require a lawman at all. He knew how lucky he was and had been for more than half his long life.

To the people of Senora and the valley the old lawman had become a fixture which somehow made them confident. His duties were simple. Each day Holt just ambulated up and down the single street touching the brim of his Stetson to each person he met.

The sheriff had craved action a couple of decades earlier when he had read a few dime novels. Then, as he slowly became older and a lot wiser, he realized that the stories he had once wished were true might in fact be really dangerous. The folks of Senora knew that the old-timer was not what he had once been but the man still had their respect. That meant a lot to everyone in the valley. They knew you had to earn respect and it could never be demanded or purchased like a sack of flour.

Will Holt had earned their respect.

He had slept for most of this hot day on the cot inside the cell of his sheriff's office. When hunger had stirred he had awoken and decided to do his evening tour of both sides of the street before stopping in the café for his supper. Over the years his supper had become delayed as his pace had slowed to half of what it had once been. But they kept the food hot for him.

Maybe it was not the actual speed at which he walked that had slowed him down but the fact that he seemed to stop and talk to everyone along the street. He knew them all and there was always something to gossip about.

Holt checked his golden hunter and then stepped out into the street. It was quite dark with only the lamplights from individual store fronts to illuminate its length. A few folks had already gone to their beds and drapes up high glowed with candle light behind their glass panes.

Holt had started to find his breathing was becoming laboured each time he reached the bottom of the street. This was an excuse for the elderly lawman to light his pipe and sit for a while outside the hardware store before crossing over and walking up the opposite side of the street to the café.

As usual the town was quiet. It was always quiet but even more so once the sun had set. There were a couple of horses tied up outside the unnamed saloon as some cowboys quenched their thirsts and played poker. A few people still moved around as they finished their daily chores. The smell of fresh baking bread drifted down from the bakery set in the back room of the café.

Everything was normal. Holt struck a match and sucked its flame into the bowl of his pipe. Smoke billowed around his head as he rested and stared out at the prairie across the river. He had seen that view for as long as he could recall and it had never before given him reason to do anything except feel satisfied.

Until now.

Sheriff Holt rubbed his white whiskers, pulled the stem of the pipe from his lips and stepped to the edge of the boardwalk. It creaked as the lawman focused on the unexpected sight which greeted his interest.

There were riders headed along the bank of the river and they were coming in his direction. That might have seemed normal as cowboys always rode across the range to Senora whenever they had a few coins in their pockets to spend, but Holt instinctively knew something was wrong.

Even with his blurred vision the lawman could tell that there were far too many horsemen for them to be from any of the ranches set in the valley. He had seen three or four riders together but there were a lot more than that kicking up dust as they steered their mounts towards the small settlement. Holt guessed that there were at least a dozen or maybe even more in the bunch. They were obviously headed towards the town.

He had no idea why, but he was troubled. Really troubled.

'Now who might that be?' Holt muttered to himself as he continued to stare out into the moonlight.

The answer to that question was getting closer with every puff of his pipe. Sheriff Will Holt's ability as an upholder of the law was about to be tested. He would not be found wanting.

ELEVEN

They had not slowed their thunderous pace since leaving the foot of the mighty waterfall and setting out for Senora. It was only when the lights of the remote settlement came into sight that Hyram Slade and his cohorts decided to stop to rest their horses in midstream. The icy waters still flowed fast and furious around the legs of their mounts as the riders surrounded their leader and awaited his merciless commands. Ahead the river was becoming shallower and broader as it raced towards a ford.

Every one of their unscrupulous eyes was on the yellow moonlight which danced across the river ahead of their snorting mounts. There was less than two miles to go before they reached the unsuspecting Senora and each of the eager horsemen had already caught its scent in his flared nostrils.

They were like a pack of ravenous wolves, eager to sink their fangs into their next prey. The callous bunch allowed their horses to drink as they checked and double-checked their individual arsenals.

It seemed as though every spare inch on and around their saddles was taken up with bags, scabbards and spare gunbelts filled with all known types of weaponry and ammunition.

The men who heralded themselves as mere honest, hard-working cowboys were far better equipped and armed than any troop of cavalry west of the Pecos. Slade ensured that.

The bitter truth was that these men were nothing more than cold-blooded rustlers who liked killing anyone who stood in their way. When you rode for Hyram Slade you reaped the rewards only dishonest souls could ever aspire to equalling. There was no profit in showing mercy. Only taking what you wanted by any means possible made the real money in the West.

Keeping his army of impatient hired guns in check, Slade reached into his deep coat-pocket and pulled out a handsome silver flask. It still bore the initials of its original owner engraved upon its gleaming side. Slade's fingers carefully unscrewed its stopper as his eyes darted at everything which lay ahead of them.

He took a long swallow of the whiskey and considered their approach to where the first of Senora's wooden structures became visible, jutted out on a rise. A forest of black trees prevented a better view of their target.

'We ride straight in,' Slade said as the hard liquor burned its way down his dry gullet. 'It'll be easy pickings.'

'Ya sure there ain't no virile young bucks up in that town, boss?' Colby asked. He was still nursing his bruised head. 'Ya certain that there is only old folks there? Right?'

Slade lowered the flask from his lips again. 'If I didn't know any better I'd think ya was scared of them old 'uns. Ain't scared, are ya, Flint?'

Colby's eyes narrowed. 'Nope. I ain't scared of no one.'

'Except me.' Slade chuckled.

The gunfighter steadied his mount and glared at his paymaster with burning hatred in his eyes. He watched as the head of the ruthless man turned on him.

'I asked ya a question, Flint. Are ya scared of me?'

'I answered ya,' Colby growled.

'I asked if ya scared of *me*. Are ya?' Slade was mocking his top gun in front of all the others and Colby knew it. Yet what was he to do? Either way he was going to lose face. 'Look at me, Flint. Are ya scared of me?'

Flint Colby gathered his reins up until his gloved hands touched his sweat-soaked shirt. 'Yep. I'm plumb scared of ya, boss. No sane critter would be anything but scared of ya.'

Satisfied, Slade turned his attention to the others. Between sips of whiskey the cruel horseman looked at each of them in turn and spewed out his orders. Each of the riders listened intently, in fear of what Slade might do to them if they made a mistake.

'This is gonna be a turkey shoot, boys,' Slade announced finally, as though the outcome of the deed was a foregone conclusion. 'There's enough of us to go from one house to the next and wipe all them varmints out. Show no mercy. Kill 'em all. Right? I don't want even one witness left sucking in air when we're finished in Senora. Not one.'

'We could have rounded up half them steers by now,' Colby said bluntly. 'This is just a waste of time and lead.'

With venom burning in his eyes Slade glanced at Colby. 'We're doing it this way 'coz I said so, Flint. Ain't having no posse following us back to the Lazy S. We kill 'em all. Ghosts can't trail nobody.'

Colby looked away.

Cass eased his horse just beyond Colby's and caught Slade's eye with a wave of his hands. 'But what about them ranchers and their hands out on the range, boss?'

The other men all nodded.

Slim Peters pulled his horse's head up out of the water with a jerk of his reins. 'Cass is right, Boss. We ain't got no idea how many cowboys there are out there. They might even outnumber us.'

106

'They'll surely come riding to Senora like hogs to a trough when the shooting starts,' Foster said. Then he spat and added, 'Then what?'

'We kill them as well, ya fool,' Slade snarled. 'Ya talking about stinking cowpunchers, not gunfighters like you boys are. I bet there ain't but one gun in each of them ranch houses over yonder. Look at the guns ya all got. Let the bastards come looking to see what the shooting is. Let 'em come. It'll be the last thing they ever does. Remember we're here to rustle up them longhorns. Nobody stands in our way. Savvy?'

Flint Colby turned his horse and looked straight at his blustering boss. 'I thought we come here to find the carcass of that drifter.'

Slade finished the whiskey and returned the silver flask to his coat pocket. His eyes flashed at Colby.

'That as well, Flint. That as well. Them steers are a bonus which will make me even wealthier than I already am.'

Brand-burner Huck Jones jabbed his spurs and moved his horse through the water ahead of all the others and pointed a finger through the tall grass upon the range. 'Look.'

They all looked.

'A rider,' Jones said.

Flint Colby rose in his stirrups, balanced and squinted. 'I see two. One a quarter-mile behind the other. They're both headed for the town damn fast.'

'Good. I wish they'd all head into town.' Slade smirked angrily. 'Saves us going looking for at least two of them cowpunchers. C'mon.'

The sixteen riders spurred and continued on.

The strange light of myriad stars and a bright moon cast an eerie hue across the range of swaying grass beyond the sparkling river. Nothing man could have manufactured would have equalled its awe-inspiring glow over the range and the land which led along the twisted course of the river towards the town of Senora. Yet the riders led by the brutal figure of Hyram Slade saw nothing ahead of their lathered mounts except another town to crush beneath the stout heels of their cowboy boots. More notches on their gun grips beckoned.

The lantern-light inside the hardware store dimmed and then went out behind the sheriff as he tapped the smouldering ash from his pipe bowl against nearest wooden upright. Senora was getting ready for another night of sleep. No one in the little town realized what was heading towards them.

Will Holt heard the footsteps find the boardwalk, turn, and then the sound of a key being inserted into the rusted old lock. The door was ritually secured. Holt did not have to turn around to see the man who had just locked up his hardware store for the night. He recognized the familiar movements of Joe Kane. They had been branded into his memory over more than twenty years.

'Joel,' the sheriff greeted him.

'What ya looking at, Will?' Kane asked. He shuffled next to the sheriff, who was staring out into the moonlight.

'Riders,' Holt replied drily. 'A whole heap of the critters by the looks of it.'

'Where?' Kane asked, rubbing shoulders with the older man. 'Where ya looking at?'

Will Holt raised the stem of his pipe and pointed. 'See them, Joe? By the river. I count me an even dozen.'

Joe Kane studied the images of the horsemen who were driving their horses with both spur and rein towards the remote settlement.

'More like fifteen or sixteen by my reckoning,' the hardware store owner contended. 'Could even be a whole lot more. I wonder who they are and how come they're headed here?'

Holt looked alarmed. 'Damn it all. That's even more troubling. I hadn't thought about why they might be coming here, Joe. Strangers heading to Senora could mean a whole wagonload of bother.'

Kane gave an assenting nod. 'Yep. A whole heap of strangers adds up to gun play in my book, Will.'

The sheriff rubbed his neck with the flat of his hand. He had not worn a gun for more than a decade. There had not been any call. Now he just might need to strap one on to his withered frame to protect the people of Senora.

'I'm heading on home, Will,' Kane said. 'I suggest ya do the same. Ain't no reason for us old 'uns to get mixed up in the makings of trouble, if that's what's coming.'

'You can go home to that fat woman of yours but I have to hang around, Joe.' Holt sighed solemnly. 'I'm the law in these parts. The only law. It's my job to stand up against vermin if'n that's what they are.'

Kane patted Holt's shoulder gently. 'Ya an old fool. What chance have you got against so many riders if'n they start causing a ruckus? They'll chew ya up and spit ya out. If I was you I'd find me a flour barrel and hide in it.'

'It's still my job to protect ya all,' the sheriff repeated. 'That's what I'm paid to do.'

Shaking his head, Joe Kane turned and started to walk along the street towards his home. 'Ya always was a fool, Will. Now ya an old fool. Don't end up a dead 'un.'

The elderly lawman was about to return to his office when his attention was drawn to another rider who was cutting straight across the vast range of high grass toward Senora. Will Holt steadied himself and stared with wide-open eyes at the horseman who could not have travelled faster if his horse's tail were alight.

'Now who in tarnation is that?' Holt wondered aloud. 'He seems to be in a real hurry to get here and no mistake.'

The sight of the solitary rider did not trouble the lawman as much as seeing the group of approaching horsemen. Whoever the man atop the powerful horse was, he was coming from the direction of one of the ranches. That at least suggested he was not looking for any trouble.

As fast as his aged legs could manage, Holt began to walk back along the boardwalk to his office to get his guns. Then, just as he reached it he heard the sound of a horse's hoofs beating upon the ground behind him. The chestnut stallion had entered the wide street. The sheriff paused and glanced over his shoulder. There was no fear in his eyes. Holt had outgrown being afraid of anything.

The sheriff did not recognize the rider but had seen the skittish horse beneath him many times. Holt rested his hands on his hips as the horseman steered the fiery animal towards the sheriff's office. The lawman whistled and caught Hardie's attention.

'Hey,' Holt called out.

Hardie drew rein and swung the stallion about. The drifter looked down at the frail man sporting the tin star.

'Are you the sheriff?' Hardie asked in disbelief.

Holt nodded slowly several times and spat at the ground between them. 'Yep. And what might ya want, stranger?'

The young horseman quickly dismounted and dragged the horse behind him until he was level with the old man. 'There's riders headed this way and I got reason to think they might be hankering to shoot this town up.'

The sheriff did not react to the statement. He looked at the horse and then at the drifter. 'Ain't that Tom Steele's horse ya got there, boy?'

'Sure is. I work for him,' Hardie answered. He pointed his free hand back at the river. 'But that ain't ya problem. Them riders are.'

'Why'd ya figure they're trouble, boy?' the sheriff asked in a calm fashion. 'How'd ya know that?'

'I know it coz they bin trying to kill me for the longest while, that's why,' Hardie explained, waving his hands around like a windmill. 'If they are the same varmints, they'll probably kill themselves a whole heap of your townsfolk.'

'Why?'

'Damned if I know.' Hardie pulled his shirt up and showed the sheriff the graze along his side. 'They done this to me with one of their Winchesters. They'd have killed me if I hadn't have got a tad lucky.'

Will Holt rubbed his whiskers. 'Who are they?'

'Damned if I know.'

'Ya don't know a damn lot, do ya?' Holt said.

The drifter looked over his shoulder. 'I know enough to be scared, Sheriff.'

The lawman gave a slight jerk of his head. 'C'mon.'

Hardie did as he was told. The lawman entered the sheriff's office and Hardie secured his reins to the hitching rail as the old man turned the lamp wheel up to illuminate the small offices interior.

'This might be real serious, sir,' Hardie stressed.

'I heard ya the first time.' The sheriff walked round his desk. He opened its top drawer and withdrew his gunbelt. 'A tad dusty but my old Remington never let me down when I was young like you still are.'

The drifter watched anxiously as Holt strapped the belt around his waist and proceeded to buckle it. 'Ya got any deputies? There's an awful lot of them critters and they all got plenty of guns.'

Holt gave out a chuckle. 'Nope. No deputies. There's just little old me.'

'Ya mean that we're alone to face them?'

'Stop fretting, boy,' Holt advised. 'We got us more than enough rifles and shells here should we need them.'

Steve Hardie looked at the rifle rack. Cobwebs linked all the dusty Winchesters together. 'When was the last time any of them carbines was oiled, Sheriff?'

Before the lawman could reply the sound of horses' hoofs filled the small office. Both men looked at one another with troubled expressions.

'They couldn't have got here yet,' Holt said as he moved to the door.

With hands on both his guns' grips, Hardie turned and moved to the shoulder of the small sheriff.

TWELVE

Tom Steele had only just reached the ford across the wide river in pursuit of Steve Hardie when suddenly a thunderous volley of lead spewed out of the rifle barrels of the approaching horsemen. The startled rancher swung his head to his right as a score of red tapers came hurtling from out of the darkness at him and his horse. The hot venom was merciless. Bullets found both him and his buckskin mount. Droplets of blood mingled with the splashing river water and hung in the moonlight.

The animal made a sickening sound beneath Steele, then crumpled in full flight into a mutilated heap. Plumes of spray fountained. The rancher was thrown headlong over the neck of his mount into an unforgiving thicket of brambles. He lay there for a few seconds with his head buried in the mud. Then he heard the sound of the riders growing louder and louder.

Though dazed and bleeding, Steele somehow managed to scramble to his feet. He staggered for a few moments and looked back along the river. His eyes focused and his heart sank. More bullets flew at him. Steele threw himself to the side beneath the deadly volley. He swallowed hard and vainly tried to lay a hand on his scattergun in the darkness.

It was nowhere to be found but the horsemen were still coming. Coming like a wall of death as they continued to fire their weaponry to where they had seen him thrown. The ground all around Steele ripped up as their bullets tore into it. He held his shoulder and then realized that it had not just been his horse who had been hit by the bullets. Yet there was no pain. Only blood. His blood.

Steele's eyes focused on the two holes in his jacket and the gleaming gore which oozed out between his fingers. His mind suddenly cleared and came out of the dazed confusion the fall had caused.

'That boy was right,' Steele muttered. This had to be the same men that the young drifter had told him about. The same men who seemed to want nothing more than to add to their tally of notches.

He was desperate. He had to escape their lead. Lead which was again getting closer as they thundered towards him.

His entire body ached. Steele knew he was too old. Too old for most things, but especially being horse-thrown. He managed to crawl up the rise to

116

where the town's solitary street began. As he reached the edge of the first of the wooden buildings another barrage of lead exploded all around him. The side wall of the building was hit just ahead of him. A million splinters of hot sawdust hit him straight in the face as his shaking legs managed to reach the wall.

His eyes were aflame. No baby could have matched the tears which streamed from his eyes. Smouldering sawdust burned into his skull. Steele screamed out in agony, then crashed into the side wall of the house he could no longer see. He fell on his back and listened fearfully to the salvo of rifle bullets as they passed over his stricken form.

Using his teeth he pulled his gloves from his hands. His fingers clawed at his eyes trying to rid them of the unbelievable misery he was enduring. But no matter how hard he tried he could not stop the pain.

The brutal pain seemed to be growing as the splinters burned like branding-irons, deeper and deeper into his eyes.

The sound of hoofs grew louder. The attackers opened up with another salvo and he heard the bullets carving their way down the wall beside him. More sawdust showered over him. Steele screamed out in agony and desperation. This was no way to die, his mind told him. Not like this. Not blinded and helpless on the ground.

117

Then a voice called at him.

'Stay there, Tom.'

Steele knew the voice. It was Steve. His arms reached up from the ground and searched for the young man.

'Don't ya move,' Hardie shouted. 'I'm coming.'

'Where are ya?' The rancher screamed out above the noise of another deafening volley of bullets as his ears listened to them tearing more wood from the wall which loomed unseen over his prostrate body. Chunks of wood cascaded over the rancher.

'Stay there.'

'Steve?' Steele's voice shrieked.

Then he felt the powerful hands of the drifter gripping his shoulders before sliding under him. Hardie scooped the helpless rancher up off the ground, turned on his heels and ran for cover a mere heartbeat before more rifle bullets cut through the darkness after them.

Steele had no way of knowing it but he was being carried like a baby across the wide street to the open door of the sheriff's office, where Will Holt stood waiting.

No sooner had the panting Hardie entered the office with his defenceless burden than the old lawman spotted the first of the riders turn into the street.

'Here they come, boy,' Holt said. He levelled his Remington at them and squeezed its trigger.

Slade and his men drew rein as the well-aimed .44 bullet plucked one of their riders off his saddle and threw him back into their dust.

'They got Luke, boss.' Foster yelled out as another of the sheriff's shots passed between their ranks.

'Take cover, ya birdbrains.' Hyram Slade leapt like a man half his age off his mount and hauled the animal between two of the buildings at the end of the street. He swung round and watched his hired guns follow suit.

Colby slapped the tail of his horse. He drew one of his guns from his holster and cocked its hammer. 'Ya said they was all old, boss. Ya said this was gonna be a turkey shoot. But Luke is lying back there calling ya a liar. He's dead and I reckon he ain't gonna be the only one before this lets up.'

Slade gritted his teeth. 'It was Slim's fault for opening up on that rider back there, Flint. Must have woked some *hombre* up from his deathbed.'

The frustrated Colby leaned around the edge of the wall and squinted hard. There were not enough lights along the street to see anything clearly. Even the moon and the stars were little help either, as storm clouds began to gather far above the valley. He bit his lip. 'How we gonna kill them now, Slade? Now they've woken up? Let's head back and just rustle up them steers like ya planned.'

'We finish this and then we rustle up them longhorns,' Slade said firmly.

'The boss is right,' Masters snarled in agreement with Slade. 'This town and everything in it is ours once we kill all these old-timers. Could be a fortune here for the taking.'

Slade looked at Huck Jones and the three men behind the brand-burner. 'Ya circle around this building and try and get level with whoever it is that's shooting at us, Huck. Blast them to hell and back.'

The four men left the main group of the gun-fighters with their paymaster and did as they were instructed.

Slim Peters still held on to his smoking Winchester as he eased himself up alongside Slade. 'Can't be more than one man firing his hogleg at us, boss.'

Another shot rang out and lit up the dark street.

'Down there.' Slade pointed the barrel of his gun in the direction of the sheriff's office. 'I seen the flash come from that building.'

'That's the sheriff's office,' Colby said. 'I can see the sign on top of the overhang.

Hyram Slade twisted as he smiled. 'If that's the same sheriff that was here the last time I rode through Senora he's gotta be over seventy if he's a day, boys. If'n he's all this town's got to protect it, I reckon this is gonna be a turkey shoot after all.'

Most of the residents of Senora had hidden themselves away when the gunplay had erupted along the normally quiet thoroughfare, but not blacksmith Olaf Ericson.

The genial giant of a man had been working at his forge bending horseshoes into shape with his usual skill when the first shots had echoed around the town. Bathed in his own sweat, the large man had lowered the tongs back into the hot embers and walked to the wide-open doors of his stable.

Perched at the very opposite end of the long street the livery stable stood as testament to the fact that this was a land full of horses. Ericson could not recall the last time he had heard shooting anywhere near Senora, and that troubled him.

The forge glowed from the well-used bellows which had fanned its belly of fire for countless hours as Olaf Ericson had worked. Now the muscular man had other things on his mind. Unlike so many others who lived in the remote town he was neither old nor a coward. As his body gleamed in the light of the red-hot forge he nodded to himself and strode powerfully back to where his anvil stood.

The big man had never possessed a gun of any description; he had always relied upon his strength and good fortune whenever trouble had raised its head.

He scratched his thinning hair and sucked in a deep breath. Not a man who ever went looking for trouble, the blacksmith had seen his fair share of it over the years he had plied his trade.

'I think that Olaf should go see who is shooting at the sheriff,' he muttered to himself in broken English, before effortlessly picking up a hefty long-handled hammer off the anvil and resting it on his brawny shoulder. 'I think then I crack a few skulls by golly.'

Untroubled by the shots which continued to resound along the town's one street, Olaf Ericson strode out of the livery stable and marched towards the rear of the buildings. He was going to find out who had disturbed his peace.

THIRTEEN

This was no longer a shoot-out. This was now a raging battle which would continue until the Grim Reaper had been paid his due. Down the street outside the saloon the two horses which were tethered to the hitching pole had tried to free themselves and were lathering up feverishly as their unarmed masters came dashing out from the drinking-hole.

The cowboys leapt over the rail. Each managed to grab his reins and tug them loose before throwing himself expertly up on to his saddle. But all either of them achieved was to give Slade and his cohorts further targets upon which to practise. The rifle bullets of both Dean Foster and Slim Peters plucked the cowboys clean off their mounts. One landed hard on the top of the hitching rail. The noise of his spine snapping filled the air. The other cowboy managed to turn his horse before the bullet tore straight through his chest and sent him limply tumbling over his cantle and crashing to the ground.

As the two wide-eyed horses galloped down the street the Slade, laughing, used his own smoking Winchester and dispatched them as well. The horses lay steaming between the sheriff's office and the merciless band of killers.

Steve Hardie left Steele on the cot inside the cell and rushed to the lawman's side. Holt was exchanging one Remington for another.

'Ya figure any other folks in this town will come to help us, Sheriff?' Hardie asked as he drew both his Colts and cocked their hammers in turn. 'The shooting must have woken them up unless they're all dead. Reckon they'll help us?'

'Maybe.' Holt shrugged and fired out towards the last place he had seen the riders before they had taken cover in the alley between the last two buildings along the street.

Hardie fired a single shot from each of his guns, then hauled the hammers back again.

'What ya mean? Ain't they got no guts? When ya hear shooting it's just natural to come looking to see if ya can help, ain't it?'

'For a young buck like you it's natural, boy,' Holt said after he had fired again. 'Not for most of the critters in Senora.'

'Why not?' Hardie fired again with both his guns. 'They yella or something?'

The sheriff glanced through the darkness at the man kneeling close to him. 'Some folks are too old. Crippled and the like. I reckon that there ain't more than a handful of six-shooters in the whole town. Folks without any guns ain't hardly likely to come anywhere close to a ruckus like this 'un.'

Hardie took a deep breath. The sheer scale of the situation was just starting to dawn upon him. 'Damn it all. Ya mean it's just you and me against the whole bunch of them?'

'Yep.' Holt sighed. 'Looks that way, don't it?'

Both men heard the sound of clumsy movement behind them. They glanced at the darkness which blanketed the cell and then saw the rancher as he staggered out into a shaft of moonlight. Steele was blinking hard but was no longer blinded.

'Ya got any spare guns in this damn place, Will?' the rancher asked.

'On the rack, Tom,' Holt answered. 'Is that blood I see on ya shoulder? Ya bin shot?'

'Yep,' Steele answered as he moved to the rack. 'It don't hurt none though. Damned strange but it just don't hurt.'

Holt looked at Hardie and winked. 'Cowboys. Ain't got the sense of the critters they ropes.'

The drifter stood and cautiously stared out into the darkness as Slade and his men returned fire yet again. The overhang shook under the violent impact of the bullets as they tore into its weathered shingles. Chunks of wood fell to the ground and the skittish stallion tore its reins free and galloped in the opposite direction.

'That horse is the most frightened critter I ever seen, Tom,' Hardie commented.

'Yep,' Steele agreed as he drew close to both men with a Winchester and box of shells in his hands. 'Gonna have to have that thing gelded. Might settle his nerves a tad.'

Hardie slid both his smoking weapons into their holsters. 'Reckon I'll get myself one of them repeating rifles off the rack, boys. Them bastards are on the limit of a six-shooter's range.'

The broad-shouldered drifter was about to leave the sheriff's side and get one of the dusty rifles for himself when he heard Holt exclaim behind him.

'What in tarnation is that?'

Hardie swung around and saw four figures creeping down the dark alleyway opposite the sheriff's office. He pushed both his comrades aside and stepped into the frame of the door as the gunfighters all fired in unison. The red tapers of potential death came speeding from the men's guns straight at him.

The tall man drew his guns, dropped to his knees then cocked and fired them at almost the same time. He saw two of the shadowy figures being buckled by his shots. He repeated the swift action again. Brand-burner Huck Jones staggered like a drunken fool out into the street. Only the light of the moon and stars showed him fall on to his lifeless face.

Suddenly more shots rang out. It was like a bombardment of revenge from Slade and his hired help. The entire front wall of the office erupted as their bullets made dust of its planks. As the drifter crawled back into the relative safety of the small office the sound of breaking glass filled his ears. Shards of shattered windowpane covered his wide back. Blood ran from those which had cut through his shirt and found his flesh. The drifter crawled to the sides of the two older men upon the floor.

'Ya blasted fool. Ya could have got killed there, Steve,' Steele scolded.

'Pull this glass out of my back, will ya?' Hardie uttered as his fingers withdrew fresh bullets from his belt and began to reload his smoking weapons. 'I finished four of the vermin, didn't I? Trouble is, that still leaves about a dozen of them.'

The rancher extracted the dagger-shaped glass fragments from Hardie's broad back and tossed them out of the door as another deafening storm of bullets ripped into the wall of the gunsmoke-filled room. Wood and plaster debris fell like hailstones all around the three men.

Hardie snapped both his gun chambers shut and holstered one of the guns as his thumb cocked the hammer of its twin. 'Is there another way out of this

127

office, Sheriff?'

'Yep.' Holt nodded and pointed at the back wall beyond the cell. 'Door to the back lane.'

Hardie brushed the debris off himself and was about to rise to his feet when the sound of a knock upon the rear door came to his and the others' ears. 'Ya hear that?'

'Who in tarnation is loco enough to come visiting at this hour?' the lawman asked. 'Ya'd think they'd wait until the shooting eased up a tad.'

Hardie sprang to his feet. He moved swiftly into the shadows and stared at the doorknob. It was turning. He gritted his teeth, then rested his painful back against the wall to the side of the door. He levelled his gun at the brass knob.

The door was not locked.

The drifter felt his throat go dry as he trained his Colt at the door and waited. It eased open and the huge shape of Olaf Ericson came into view.

'Sheriff?' Olaf whispered as though afraid he might offend someone by talking normally. 'This is Olaf. I want to know if I can help?'

All three of the men inside the office gave out a sigh of relief.

'Git in here, Olaf,' Holt ordered the huge man.

Like a well-brought-up child the blacksmith obeyed. He was about to venture to the bullet-ridden front of the building when another hail of gunfire ripped even more of the porch apart.

Hardie placed a hand on the big man's muscular arm. Their eyes met. They both nodded.

'I'd stay away from that particular door if'n I was you, friend,' Hardie suggested. 'Even a blind man couldn't miss anyone as large as you are.'

'Can Olaf help, Sheriff?'

The three men looked at the sweating black-smith, who stood holding his hefty long-handled hammer in his left hand as if it weighed little more than a feather.

'Ya got a gun?' Hardie asked.

Olaf shook his head. 'I no like guns. I got me my hammer though. I go crush some skulls for ya?'

Sheriff Holt gave him a grateful smile. 'Ya go home, Olaf. I knows ya means well but them varmints down yonder would shoot ya faster than spitting out a lump of baccy.'

'But Olaf want to help,' the blacksmith insisted.

The drifter patted the muscular shoulder of the man. 'A hammer against gunfighters is suicidal, boy.'

Olaf looked indignant. 'I help. Ya cannot stop me. I help.'

There was no way of arguing with anyone as large as Olaf Ericson and they all knew it. They watched as he turned and stormed back out into the dark lane. Hardie rested a hand on the doorknob.

'What ya thinking about, boy?' Holt asked.

Steve Hardie glanced at both of the kneeling

men. 'There ain't no way we can win this by cowering in here like whipped dogs. I gotta try and get behind them. Draw them out from their cover and then. . . .'

Steele did not say a word.

'Are ya sure? Out there ya might just find they got the advantage of numbers, boy,' the lawman ventured. 'Gotta be close to a dozen of the critters still living. Bad odds.'

'Least I got me some guns and I know how to use them,' the drifter said firmly. 'If that Olaf has got the guts to face them with only a damn hammer, then I can sure try and end this with my .45s.'

Steele glanced at the young man. 'Are ya sure?'

Hardie nodded. 'Yep.'

The rancher cranked the rifle. 'Keep alert, Steve. Them *hombres* out there don't take prisoners.'

'Neither do I, Tom,' Hardie assured him before disappearing into the darkness behind the besieged office.

The sheriff scrambled across the glass-littered floor and closed and secured the rear door. Then he turned and stared at the wounded rancher. 'Look at us, Tom. Two old 'uns against an army of locobeans.'

Steele had loaded the rifle in his grip. 'Yep.'

'They don't know who they're messing with.' Holt sniffed and made his way back to his companion.

'Sure enough, Will. They'd be mighty scared if

they knew who they was up against.' Steele fired the Winchester and cranked its mechanism again, sending a brass casing flying back over his shoulder.

'I figure they'd be shaking in their boots.'

'Damn right.'

Both men continued firing up into the gun-smoke.

FOURTEEN

Steve Hardie had run the length of the back alley behind the wooden buildings before he came to a grinding halt and realized that however large the massive Olaf Ericson was he had simply vanished. The drifter holstered both his guns and ran his hands over his sweating face. His eyes darted up and down the shadowy expanse but he could not see the blacksmith anywhere.

'Damn it all. Where'd he go?' Hardie cursed in a hushed tone. 'That big critter might have bin real useful.'

Suddenly a noise to his right alerted his senses. Hardie swung on his heels and crouched. His heart was racing. He tried to swallow but there was no spittle in his dry throat. Only choking fear.

Then he heard it again.

Now he was afraid. He had never been more afraid in all his days. There were many men in town who appeared to have nothing on their collective mind but killing. To Hardie it made absolutely no sense. He had fought many men in his time but there had always been a reason. A damn good reason. These men were not fighting. They were killing for no reason. They were merciless. That was totally alien to everything by which the drifter had lived his life. There was an unwritten code inside him which he had never deviated from and yet these men just wanted to kill.

His mind raced to match his pounding heart.

The drifter moved cautiously towards the sound. He had to find out what had made it. Men like Hardie did not turn and run away from their fears. They faced them head on.

A million thoughts filled his mind.

Maybe it was some of the riders who had decided to attack the innocent Senora. Perhaps they were prowling in order to find easier prey than that which had opposed them from Will Holt's office.

It might be Olaf.

The noise filled his ears again. This time it was a lot louder. Closer. Whatever was making the sound, it was getting closer.

Hardie took a deep breath, steadied himself and walked towards the darkest of the shadows. He knew that every step might be taking him closer towards his own brutal death but he kept on walking anyway, towards more of the gunfighters, who seemed intent on nothing more than a lethal slaying.

This time it might be his turn to run out of luck.

He reached the last corner.

The aroma of the livery stable filled his flared nostrils. Then something moved in the blackest of the shadows less than ten feet from where he had paused.

Hardie drew both his guns at lightning speed and aimed their black barrels at the shadows.

'Ya better show that stinking carcass of yours or I'll surely kill ya,' the drifter warned. 'Come here slow and easy.'

He heard movement coming towards him. Step by step it was approaching just as he had demanded.

Terror engulfed him. Every sinew in his body wanted to squeeze the triggers of his .45s before it was too late. Kill before being killed, but that was too easy. Only a coward fired a gun without knowing who or what they were aiming at. Hardie realized that unseen guns might already be aimed at him but he held his nerve.

He would not allow himself to fire his weapons blindly. He had to see who it was who was coming straight at him.

Then his question was answered.

The sight of the skittish chestnut stallion made him lean back against the wall of the building and sigh heavenwards. His heart started to beat normally once more as the horse pushed its bridled head into his heaving chest. He holstered his Colts and grabbed hold of the reins.

'Ya lucky I ain't a yella-belly, boy,' Hardie whispered into the horse's ear. 'Otherwise I'd have made glue of ya.'

The storm clouds had now filled half the sky. The moon valiantly tried to send its eerie illumination down upon those who dwelled beneath its magnificence. Yet it only succeeded for part of the time as the clouds raced across the heavens.

The men who still clung to the presence of their crazed leader moved along in a line as Slade led them into the depths of the dark alleys. His throat was sore from having vainly called out to Jones and the trio of other gunmen. Even though the ruthless ranch owner had heard the roaring fury of lead which had been exchanged little more than five minutes earlier, Slade was not convinced that Huck Jones and his three companions could have possibly lost their confrontation with the unseen gunman who had drawn and fired his Colts so expertly across the wide street from the porch of the sheriff's office.

It was obvious to the others that four of their number were dead but not to Slade. Slade refused to accept death unless he actually saw it before him. Saw the blood for himself.

Shadows lurked phantomlike behind the buildings and an acrid scent hung in the air as the eleven hardened gunfighters carefully negotiated their way around the outhouses. Hyram Slade was first to reach the narrow lane between the wooden buildings which were situated directly opposite the embattled sheriff's office. Half the wooden shingles had either been shot off the porch overhang or had fallen through force of gravity once enough lead had eaten away at the fabric of the structure. There was no glass left in the façade of the office, neither was any of its planking without smouldering bullet holes riddling its form.

Smoke from the guns of whoever it was inside the office still hung low in the air. Defiantly Will Holt and Tom Steele kept firing up the street at well-timed intervals.

Yet Slade did not see or hear any of this.

All his narrowed eyes could see were the four crumpled bodies of the men he had sent to this place to get the drop on whoever it was who had been holding them at bay. Slade felt a rage engulfing his very soul. Nobody did this to him or any of the men he still regarded as his property. Blood clung to the soles of his boots as he backed away from the carnage in the lane. Even the shadows could not hide his fury.

'Nobody does this to my men,' Slade growled. His head began to pound more insistently the angrier he became. His fingers pressed into his temples in an attempt to stop the pain. 'Nobody. I don't allow no killing of my men.'

'They're all dead,' Dan Foster said after inspecting each of the corpses laid out where Steve Hardie's bullets had dropped them. 'Each of them done for with a single shot, boss.'

Slade clenched his fist and chewed on his knuckles. 'That's plumb impossible. Ain't nobody can kill that easy.'

Flint Colby knelt and turned one of the bodies over. He looked at it carefully. He then moved to the next and repeated his actions.

'Dan's right, boss,' Colby said, and stood upright once more. 'One shot to the heart. They all got plugged with just one shot each.'

Slade edged closer to his top gun. His head leaned across until it almost rested on Colby's shoulder. His words were softly spoken as though he feared that the others might overhear him. 'Ain't possible is it, Flint? Who can shoot like that in these parts?'

Colby shook his head. 'It don't seem possible but the evidence is there. I ain't never seen such accuracy in all my days, boss. Whoever done this is the best damn shootist I ever seen.'

The brooding Slade moved away from Colby. He stood in the darkness between the two buildings and the sheriff's office and looked down the long lane. The two unseen figures were still firing their weapons.

'Can't have bin that old sheriff that done this,' Slade said as though trying to convince himself of something he was unsure about. 'He could never have done this. Ain't possible, is it?'

'Then who?' Slim Peters asked nervously.

'There gotta be someone else mixed up in this,' Slade concluded firmly. 'Someone we ain't never run into before. A real top gun.'

'Someone I sure ain't hankering to meet up with,' Colby admitted. 'If he can do that kinda shooting in the dark, just think of what he could do with his guns in the daylight.'

The men who surrounded Slade in the blackness of the alley seemed to be getting more and more nervous as they contemplated the situation their leader had led them into.

'I'm for high-tailing it out of here, boss,' Ty Masters said.

'That goes for me as well,' another of the gunmen said, nodding. 'I don't wanna end up like these boys.'

Soon all of them had spoken with the exception of Colby. They agreed that the wisest thing to do was ride. Ride away from something and someone of whom they knew they could not get the better. But Hyram Slade was not wise. He never had been. He was just burning with rage.

'Let's high-tail it, boss,' Masters repeated.

A furious Slade pointed an accusing finger straight at the brand-burner. 'Changed ya tune mighty quick there, Ty. A minute or so back ya was all for us razing this town to the ground and filling our pockets with whatever loot we found when the gunsmoke cleared. Now ya wanna run. Run like a scared jack rabbit. Ya yella, boy. Plumb yella.'

Masters moved back. 'That ain't fair. How was I to know we was up against a real marksman? Whoever done for Huck and the boys must be the best shot in the West.'

'I pay ya all to be the best shots in the West,' the rancher snarled at Masters. 'Earn ya keep or I'll plug ya all myself. Do ya savvy?'

Peters rubbed his neck. 'But we ain't got any notion of who or what this *hombre* is, boss. All we know is he can shoot up a storm. How can we get the better of him?'

'To hell with him. We gotta kill all the folks in Senora and then we'll be sure of getting him as well. Right?' Slade raged. 'Ya do what we come here to do. There's gotta be a fortune in this town stuffed under mattresses. Ya wanna share that between ya or just run scared and leave it?'

The gunfighters knew that some men could never quit once they had started something. Hyram Slade was such a man. Pride or insanity had always driven him on. Now his beleaguered followers began to realize that there was a high price to pay for accepting wages from such a unstable creature.

Colby was thoughtful and quiet. He had listened to them all and not uttered a word. Even though he knew the sensible thing to do was agree with the others, something inside him still feared the man who paid his salary.

'What do you figure is the best thing to do, Flint?' Dan Foster asked the silent Colby.

'Like the boss said, it ain't finished yet,' Colby replied without looking up at any of them. 'Huck was a pal of mine and I aim to wipe the whole bunch of these townsfolk out to get even.'

'Ya loco, Flint,' Peters said with a sigh.

'I'm doing what Slade tells me to do,' Colby said.

The gunfighters were stunned by the statement. None of them could fathom why Colby was siding with Slade, especially after the rancher had done his best to humiliate the tall figure all day and into the night. Yet if he was willing to stick by the raging rancher, then there had to be a reason. A reason which Colby had yet to reveal.

'Fine, Flint. That's mighty fine,' Slade patted Colby on the shoulder and nodded. 'We'll show these youngsters that I'm right.'

Colby showed no interest as he pushed bullets from his coat into the magazine of his Winchester. He glanced up at the others and winked. 'Yep. Me and the boys will be right behind ya all the way, boss. Ain't that right, boys?'

Each of the men standing between the rancher and Colby nodded like puppets having their strings pulled.

Satisfied, Slade led the confused gunfighters to the rear of one of the buildings they were standing beside, then he looked upward. There was a small window close to the eaves. No bigger than a bootbox. He pointed at it and cupped his hand to one of his ears.

'Hear that?'

The curious gunfighters listened.

At first they did not hear anything. Then they too heard the sound of females crying in terror. Slade turned. A break in the clouds far above Senora allowed the moonlight to illuminate his determined features. He was grinning again. 'Women. Weeping up a storm kinda women. Can ya hear them?'

Half the men nodded whilst the others just stared up at the high window. Slade led them further round the back of the building, then stopped when he found what he was looking for. The rear door had seen better days. Its hinges were barely keeping it within its frame. Slade took hold of its handle and eased the door towards him.

'Well I'll be. How'd ya know it wouldn't be locked, boss?' Peters asked.

Slade glanced at his followers. His smile was even more sickening than previously. 'Townsfolk like these never lock their doors. They ain't never heard of critters like us.'

'What ya figuring on doing?' Masters wondered as a dozen possibilities came flashing into his

141

depraved mind. 'We gonna go up there and have us some fun? I ain't had me no female company since I don't know when.'

Slade gave a slow calculated nod. 'In a way, Ty. I reckon that we'll never get them men inside the sheriff's office to show their faces unless they see us holding some females hostage.'

'Ya gonna tempt them varmints out of the sheriff's office by making them think we'll kill their females if'n they don't give themselves up, boss?' Colby asked as he cradled his rifle under his armpit.

Slade cupped Colby's rugged and bruised face in the palms of his hands as he nodded frenziedly. 'Exactly, Flint boy. Then when they show themselves we shoot them.'

'What about the women?' Masters probed.

'We kill them as well,' Slade added.

'Before or after I have me some fun, boss?'

Slade shrugged. 'I never knew ya was so fussy, Ty.'

'He ain't.' Foster spat. 'Dead or alive, womenfolk is all the same to him.'

Colby looked at the others. 'Sounds like a darn good plan to me, boys. Reckon we'll have us some dead heroes before the night is much older.'

'You and you and you.' The crazed rancher pointed to Peters, Masters, Foster and a couple of the others. Then he pulled the rear door of the building wide open and gestured for them to enter. 'Kill any men up there but make sure ya force the females out on to the balcony and make a whole heap of noise doing so. I want them bastards inside that office to know exactly what'll happen if they don't heed ya threats. Right?'

The five eager gunmen mumbled their agreement and then rushed inside the dark house. Within seconds the sound of hysterical screaming could be heard coming from an upper room. Colby glanced around at the remaining gunfighters. Without the five who had just entered the house there were now only four of them left apart from Slade and himself. Colby did not like the way the odds were panning out.

He looked at his paymaster long and hard.

'Where we gonna go, boss?' he asked.

'A place that offers us a clear view of that damn office, Flint. C'mon,' Slade answered. He led the others along the back of the house until they reached the next alley, which separated the house from the saloon.

Even in the lane the smell of stale sawdust and liquor filled the air. These unsavoury fumes were only matched by those emanating from the saloon's well-used outhouse.

Cass moved forward. 'We gonna hole up in there, boss? I could sure use a few stiff drinks right about now.'

'Me too,' another of the gunfighters called Brody said.

'This ain't a situation to get liquored up in,' Colby voiced his concern. 'Even sober this deal is likely to go sour on us and you knows it, boss.'

'Ya fret too much, Flint,' Slade said. 'A few whiskeys ain't gonna dull our edge on these towns-folk.'

'I'm still fretting about who it was that done for Huck and the others,' Colby replied. 'By my figuring, he's still on the loose.'

'We are gonna go in there, ain't we?' Cass asked again.

Slade grinned. 'Yep. We're gonna take over this saloon. Kill two birds with one stone as the old saying goes. We'll have us a belly full of whiskey and then train our guns on the porch of the sheriff's office and wait for them gallant critters to step out and give themselves up.'

'And then kill them,' Brody joked.

'Damn right,' Slade agreed with a snort. Then he led his men into the back of the saloon. 'C'mon. I got cactus growing in my throat.'

Sheriff Will Holt had been perfectly correct when he had said that there were probably fewer than a half-dozen firearms within the boundaries of Senora, but one of those deadly weapons had rested beneath the long mahogany bar counter inside the saloon for decades.

Barkeep Poke Carter had worked inside the saloon for all of that time and until this night had never ever placed a hand upon the dusty twin-barrelled scattergun. But that had all changed when he had witnessed the brutal slayings of the two terrified cowboys as they fled from the saloon and tried to mount their horses. The constant gunfire which had preceded the slaughter of his best customers had also lit a fuse inside the belly of the bartender. Carter had once been a man whom few tangled with. Now it was as though twenty or more years had been wiped from his slate and he was ready to prove his worth once more.

Death might be stalking the streets of Senora but it had not reckoned upon him challenging it to one last duel. If it wanted him he would not submit lightly. Carter would take as many of the town's intruders with him as he could.

He would not die alone.

The bartender had loaded the scattergun with two cartridges of buckshot and was lying prostrate behind an upturned card table close to the swing doors. The sawdust-covered floor he rested upon hid a multitude of sins. With the long double-barrelled weapon clutched in his sweating hands, Carter wondered how much blood might be added to it before too long.

Then Carter heard them. They had come through the rear door just as he had hoped they would. Straight towards his cobweb-covered shotgun.

The merciless bunch led by the arrogant Slade

burst into the main room of the seemingly empty saloon with their weaponry drawn in readiness. Seeing the array of whiskey bottles stacked upon the shelf beyond the long bar counter they spread out. Only Colby held back as though sensing the trouble to come.

Every movement was being observed by the sweat-soaked Carter, fifteen feet away from the bar counter. There were too many chairs and tables between the bartender's shotgun barrels and the gunfighters. His index finger stroked the twin triggers of the doughty weapon as he secretly prayed for the conscienceless men to come into full view.

Slade made his way round the bar counter and plucked bottles of whiskey off the long shelf that ran in front of a long mottled mirror.

'Drink ya fill, boys,' Slade bade his men confidently. He placed the bottles down and watched his men eagerly rush to them. 'Looks like we scared everyone off before they even seen us.'

Poke Carter eased himself slightly forward. The barrels of the large weapon in his hands poked out from the side of the inverted table. He had a clear shot at them, he told himself. All they had to do was turn to face him and he knew he could wipe them all out.

With his cocked and primed Winchester still under his armpit Colby raised one of the bottles and tugged its cork from its neck with his teeth. Before he had time to spit the cork away his keen eyes spotted, reflected in the mirror, movement at the far end of the saloon.

It was the movement of a twin-barrelled shotgun.

Colby dropped the bottle and swung around with the rifle at hip level. 'Duck, boys.' he screamed out to his cohorts.

But it was too late.

Like bemused steers heading into a slaughter-house, the gunfighters just turned to see what Colby was aiming his Winchester at.

All they saw was the brilliant white flash as both barrels of the scattergun unleashed their fury. It would be the last thing any of them would ever see. Flesh and gore was ripped from the men as they were torn to shreds before Slade's and Colby's unbelieving eyes. Shielded by the bar counter, Slade saw the full force of the buckshot destroy the four men standing less than three feet from him. Colby had thrown himself into a pile of stacked chairs as Cass and the others were being obliterated.

Blood covered the far wall. Lumps of flesh clung to the faded wallpaper before dropping into the sawdust.

Having sensed the imminent danger Colby had somehow managed to avoid the bloody buckshot. With his rifle still in his hands the gunfighter lay on the ground. He was dazed yet recognized the sound of the scattergun being reloaded.

'Ya OK, Flint?' Slade screamed out through the choking gunsmoke as he drew both his guns and cocked their hammers.

'Yep,' Colby called back.

'Not for long ya ain't.' Poke Carter jumped to his feet and fired one barrel of his smoking weapon straight at the bar. The buckshot blasted a huge chunk of wood out of the mahogany counter. Slade was showered in the debris and staggered backwards before falling on to the floorboards. Carter turned the rifle towards where he had heard Colby's voice. He saw the crouching gunman behind the shattered chairs, trying to get back to his feet. 'Now it's your turn to die.'

Before the barkeep had time to squeeze the other trigger he saw Colby roll over until he was clear of the splintered wood. To his horror he saw the Winchester in his hands.

'No!' Carter yelled fearfully.

Flint Colby aimed and fired within a mere heartbeat. The bullet cut through the gunsmoke and hit the barkeep in his chest. The brutal impact was enough to send Carter hurtling back until he fell into the green baize of the upturned card table. The scattergun blasted another blinding shot upwards as it hit the floor. Plaster showered down over the unblinking Carter, who lay dead in the sawdust. Blood spread out in a neat circle around the body.

Colby leant upon the bar and grabbed at a bottle

of whiskey. He pulled its cork and took a long swig of the fiery liquor. Then he glanced at his boss, who was getting back to his feet.

'Four more of our boys gone, Slade,' the gun-fighter said. He took another mouthful of the whiskey. 'This is getting kinda high-priced.'

Hyram Slade leapt over the bar and landed in the crimson mess that was all that was left of Cass, who had taken the full impact of the bartenders scatter-gun. Slade drew one of his guns, cocked its hammer and defiantly strode through the bloody sawdust to where Poke Carter's lifeless body lay beside his smoking weapon.

The rancher kicked the table aside, then emptied all six of his bullets into the head of the bartender.

'Why'd ya do that?' Colby asked. 'He was already dead. I seen to that.'

Slade glanced back at Colby. 'Now I seen to it as well.'

The gunfighter pushed the hand-guard of his Winchester down and then back up in a swift, fluent action. The spent brass casing flew from the rifle's magazine and landed in the gory mess that stretched along the length of the bar.

Neither man spoke. Neither had anything to say that had not already been said. Slade reloaded the Colt then holstered it before the gunfighter reached his side.

Then they heard the sound of the screaming

149

females. The remaining five members of their band had hauled the terrified women out of the building on to its high balcony.

'C'mon,' Slade said.

Colby grabbed hold of the rancher's arm and pulled him back from the swing doors. 'Reckon it'll be a whole lot safer if we use the back door and circle up around the lane, boss.'

'What?' Slade looked confused.

'Whoever done for Huck and the others up the street might be out there watching the front of this saloon,' Colby suggested. He rested the Winchester on his shoulder. 'We'd make damn easy targets if we just rushed on out blindly into the street.'

Hyram Slade reluctantly nodded.

'You're right, Flint.'

Both men reloaded their weapons, turned and walked across the scarlet-coloured sawdust towards the back door of the saloon. Gore stuck to their boots as they negotiated their way across the remnants of those who, only moments earlier, had been their cohorts.

They crept like vermin out into the darkness.

Long before Slater's henchmen had dragged the two battered and bruised women from their bedrooms and out on to the rickety balcony, Ty Masters and his four equally depraved companions had not only humiliated but also violated them. Even for

men who were used to paying for their carnal plea-
sures, what they had subjected the females to had
been little other than barbaric.

Blood covered the faces of both the spinster
sisters. Their nightgowns were torn, revealing
bodies unseen by anyone apart from themselves for
decades. More blood traced down the inside of the
legs of one of the sisters from her injuries. For
respectable women aged somewhere in their fifties
this had to be a fate worse than death.

They had been raped. Not by one but by all of the
five men who now used them as shields on the
balcony of their home. The calls of the gunfighters
who had satisfied their villainous urges on their
helpless victims hung on the night air as Masters,
Foster and the others mocked their unseen enemies
in the sheriff's office.

It was obvious what they wanted. They wanted
Holt and Steele to throw out their weapons and be
resigned to their fate. Either that or the two women
would pay the ultimate price for their defiance.

'Give it up, Sheriff. Throw out ya guns and come
on out with ya hands held high or these two old
women are gonna get bullets in their skulls. Savvy?
Do ya savvy, Sheriff?' Slim Peters had the loudest
voice and used it well. His every word stabbed
through the smoke-filled street and penetrated the
hearing of both Steele and Holt as they listened to
the demands.

The wily old lawman rested his bony spine against the splintered doorframe and stared at his companion. It was a troubled Tom Steele who knelt holding his smoking Winchester in his hands.

'Ya figure they'll kill old Sarah and Mary like they say, Will?' Steele asked. 'Do ya?'

Holt opened the chambers of the Remingtons on his lap and then shook the spent casings on to the floor. He began to reload his guns thoughtfully.

Steele edged closer to the sheriff. 'I'm talking to ya, Will. Do ya reckon that scum will do what they're threatening to do to the Taylor sisters?'

The sheriff sighed. 'Yep. They'll surely kill 'em if we don't do like they say and give ourselves up, Tom. Satisfied?'

'Nope.' Steele spat the acrid taste of gunsmoke from his mouth and began to reload his repeating rifle with shells from the cardboard box beside his left leg. 'I ain't for quitting this, Will. I figure they'll kill us and them old gals whatever we do. Even if we do what they demand we'll all still end up dead.'

Holt nodded. 'That's my figuring as well. Trouble is I can't think of nothing we can do. I've known them gals all their lives and I can't just let them die coz I'm feared of dying myself.'

Steele glanced up and looked out of the shattered window. His still-burning eyes spotted something down the street in the shadows. The rancher got up on to both knees and squinted hard.

He then grabbed hold of the sheriff's skinny arm and shook it excitedly.

'Look. Look down there, Will. What ya see?'

Sheriff Holt looked to where his friend was pointing and gasped in total disbelief. 'Well I'll be damned.'

With reins gripped in his teeth, Steve Hardie was galloping down the street astride Steele's powerful stallion with both guns drawn.

He had nearly reached the two dead cowboy horses lying in the centre of the wide thoroughfare when the five men on the balcony turned their weaponry upon him.

The Taylor sisters began to scream again as Ty Masters led his cohorts in opening up with their arsenal at the approaching horseman. Suddenly the street became filled with deafening blasts of deadly lead. It cut through the darkness like rods of lightning at Hardie.

The drifter stood in his stirrups as the stallion leapt over one of the carcasses. As the hoofs of his mount landed Hardie raised both arms and fired his .45s. With lethal accuracy Slim Peters was hit by both of the drifter's bullets. He flew backwards and crashed into one of his fellow outlaws. Peters lurched, tumbled over the white rail and fell to the street below.

Hardie fired again and hit another of the men. He then spat the reins from his mouth, swung his right leg over the head of the galloping stallion and, just as he reached the foot of the Taylors' house, jumped to the ground.

Bullets rained all around the drifter, who rolled over the hard ground until he reached the boardwalk below the balcony.

Seeing two of their abusers drop in bloody heaps the Taylor spinsters suddenly had renewed faith. The sisters clawed at the men who had been using them as shields and fought their way back inside the bedroom window just as another bullet came bursting through the wooden boards they were standing upon. Another gunfighter yelled out as Hardie's bullet cut through his right boot. He fell to his knees as the bewildered Foster and Masters tried to locate their valiant attacker.

Then they saw Slade and Colby emerge from the lane next to the saloon up the street. Both gunmen vainly called out.

Hardie was breathing hard as he pressed himself against the wall of the house and looked upwards at the balcony, trying to work out where to aim his next shot.

The huge hand that found the drifter's shoulder sent a cold chill racing up Hardie's spine. Had one of his foes managed to escape his attack and turn the tables on him? Hardie spun on his heels faster than even he could have imagined possible with both guns gripped in his hands. Then he saw the familiar face of the brawny blacksmith standing beside him with his long-handled hammer resting upon his muscular shoulder.

'Olaf.' Hardie sighed.

The blacksmith nodded and raised his huge hammer, holding its handle in his mighty grip. He looked like a quarryman ready to crack granite.

'I would stand back if I were you, by golly,' Ericson said as his muscular arms raised the hefty hammer back and then swung it with mighty force at the nearer of the porch's uprights.

The wooden four by four shattered as the head of the hammer smashed straight through it. The balcony gave a groan and started to lean. Before any of the gunmen standing upon it could do anything, the huge Olaf had run to the opposite end of the porch and smashed his massive hammer into the other wooden upright. It too was cut in half.

The balcony came crashing down. A cloud of dust rose up. The three hired guns hit the ground hard. Foster managed to turn and fire one of his Colts at the blacksmith. Hardie blasted his .45s at all three of them. It took only three of his bullets to silence them all.

Olaf was smiling as Hardie walked towards him. 'Have we got them all, little man?'

Before Hardie could answer the sound of another shot rang out and echoed all around him. To his horror he saw the huge man's face suddenly go blank.

Olaf fell like an axed tree at his feet.

FINALE

The sight of the dead blacksmith left the young drifter utterly stunned. Hardie stared in shock down at the huge Olaf lying at his feet. Then he saw the well-placed bullet hole. A fine whisper of smoke came from the hole as blood began to spread into the dead man's sweat-soaked shirt. Then there was a hail of more bullets, each of them was aimed straight at him.

The heat of the lead as it passed within inches of him made the startled Hardie look up. Then he buckled as one of the shots found its mark. He staggered and felt the gun in his right hand drop from his bloody fingers. His narrowed gaze darted up the street to where two men were standing close to the dead horses that lay outside the saloon. Hardie raised the gun in his left hand as more bullets came from the barrels of Colby's and Slade's weapons. One of them hit him hard.

The drifter managed to squeeze the trigger as he fell down in the dusty street. His shot flew up at the stormclouds. Pain suddenly skewered through his entire body.

He had been hit, he told himself. Hit twice. At least twice. Hardie landed on his side. Every last gasp of wind seemed to be kicked from out of his body. His eyes stared along the street past the bodies of Slade's henchmen, at the two figures who were walking towards him: walking and firing their guns as though defying him to respond.

But the drifter could not respond. He could not raise the gun off the ground and fire it again. The ground all around him was kicked up as bullet after bullet taunted him.

'Who are ya?' Slade screamed as he paused and trained both his six-shooters at the helpless man.

Colby said nothing. He just cradled his Winchester in his hands.

Then Hyram Slade's expression changed. He took two more steps forward. He was directly above the prostrate Hardie. He was staring down at the face he knew he had briefly seen before. Once before, up near the waterfall.

'It's you. You're the drifter,' Slade said.

Flint Colby moved to his paymaster's side and looked down at the bleeding Hardie. He kicked the Colt .45 aside. 'Ya right, boss. This is the stinking *hombre* we chased up to the top of the cliffs.'

Hardie tried to get up but Colby placed a boot on the drifter's bloody shoulder. He relished the sight of the pain which etched across Hardie's face.

Slade leaned over. 'Who are ya? What's ya name?'

There was no time for the drifter to reply even if he had been able. The sound of the two Remingtons blasting from inside the sheriff's office filled the street. Slade was knocked off his feet and crashed into the bodies of Foster and Masters. He was as dead as they were.

Colby had felt the bullet carve into his guts but refused to drop. He swung around and aimed his Winchester straight at the frail lawman in the door-frame and fired. The bullet might have found a larger man with meat on his bones but came nowhere near Will Holt.

The sheriff fired both his guns again. This time his aim was true and lethal. Colby twisted, then fell into the bloody dust beside the wounded Hardie.

By the time the pair of old men had reached the injured Hardie, Kate Steele had led the twenty or more cowboys into the smoke-filled street. She dismounted quickly and managed to reach the drifter before any of the others. She lifted his head off the ground and glanced at his wounds.

'Reckon he'll live, Kate?' Tom Steele asked his daughter.

She nodded with tear-filled eyes. 'He'll live, Pa. I ain't gonna let him die. I just ain't.'

Steve Hardie forced a smile. He raised his bloody hand and patted her arm. 'That mean I still got the job, Kate?'

Her lips found his, then she glanced at her father and the sheriff. 'Why'd ya let him get shot for, Pa?'

'I'm sorry, girl.' Steele shrugged as all fathers shrug when scolded by their daughters.

Hardie felt many hands help him back up to his feet. Kate alone acted as his support, though. She steadied him as the young man glanced around the street at the mayhem which surrounded them. Then he looked down at Slade's body.

'That critter called me a drifter.' Hardie repeated the words of the crazed rancher. 'Maybe that's what I am. A drifter.'

Kate reached up, grabbed his chin and turned his head until his eyes were looking straight into hers.

'Not any more ya ain't. I ain't ever letting ya out of my sight again,' she told him. 'OK?'

'OK.' Steve Hardie smiled.